THE KID FROM COURAGE

BY

RON BERMAN

www.scobre.com
www.thekidfromcourage.com

Scobre Press Corporation
2255 Calle Clara
La Jolla, CA 92037

Scobre Press books may be purchased for educa-
tional, business or sales promotional use.

First Scobre edition published 2003.

"The Dream Series," Volume 8 of 24

Edited by Debra Ginsberg
Copyedited by Gina Zondorak
Cover Art by Larry Salk
Cover Layout by Michael Lynch

ISBN 0-9708992-2-X

www.scobre.com

To all the dreamers...

We at Scobre Press are proud to bring you Volume 8 of our "Dream Series." In case this is your first Scobre book, here's what we're all about: the goal of Scobre is to influence young people by entertaining them with books about athletes who act as role models. The moral dilemmas facing the athletes in a Scobre story run parallel to situations facing many young people today. After reading a Scobre book, our hope is that young people will be able to respond to adversity in their lives in the same heroic fashion as do the athletes depicted in our books.

This book is about Bryan Berry, the Kid from Courage. Born and raised in a small town, he wonders if his dreams of tennis stardom are farfetched and unattainable. But when he develops an unlikely friendship with an old tennis coach, he discovers that old school values haven't gone out of style.

The Kid from Courage offers an in-depth look at the world of a junior tennis player-the training, the competition, and the ups and downs of trying to succeed in one of the most challenging sports in the world.

We invite you now to come along with us, sit down, get comfortable, and read a book that will dare you to dream. Scobre dedicates this book to all the people who are chasing down their own dreams. We're sure that Bryan will inspire you to reach for the stars.

Here's Bryan..."The Kid from Courage."

For Milt

CHAPTER ONE

THE KING OF COURAGE HIGH

"Ladies and gentlemen," Jimmy bellowed, glancing from side to side at an imaginary crowd, "the championship match is set to begin! Players ready?"

"Bring it on," I called out, ignoring my friend's usual theatrics. I took a deep breath, trying to convince myself that there was no reason to feel any pressure. After all, I wasn't supposed to beat the best player at Courage High. Jimmy was a year older and I was only a fourteen-year-old freshman. I reminded myself to relax and play with confidence.

As our practice match got under way, Jimmy hit a spin serve that bounced shoulder high, immediately putting me on the defensive. I tried to counter with an aggressive return, but my backhand landed just beyond the service line, much shorter than I had intended. Quickly moving forward, Jimmy loaded up his big lefty forehand and ripped the ball crosscourt for an outright winner.

I knew that Jimmy Ellis didn't take tennis—or anything else—seriously, but it was undeniable that he was a great athlete. As the match progressed, he hit a dazzling assortment of well-placed, penetrating shots, seemingly at will. Although I did manage to string a couple of good games together late in the match, I was unable to overcome Jimmy's sheer power and skill on the tennis court. The scores were 6-1, 6-2.

After crushing a serve right down the middle for a clean ace to seal the victory, Jimmy strolled lazily up to the net and shook my outstretched hand.

"You were hitting the ball pretty good out there, Bryan. I'm gonna have to keep my eye on you." He was always being sarcastic.

"Yeah, right, you were just toying with me, as usual. Dude, if you started working hard on your game, you could probably hang with the best sixteen-year-olds in the nation." It was true, he had so much potential, but tennis didn't seem to be much of a priority for him.

Jimmy grinned widely, "You sound just like my dad." Reaching into his tennis bag, he retrieved his Kansas Jayhawks baseball cap and put it on, partly covering up his blonde, unkempt hair. Jimmy's wild, ever-changing hairstyles were legendary at Courage High. Also contributing to his fashionably disheveled image was a very thin, scruffy-looking goatee.

We were a true study in contrast. With my clean-cut features and short brown hair, I had a look that could best be described as neat and stylish, maybe even a bit nerdy. Of greater importance was my slight, five-foot-eight-inch frame, which was clearly in need of some strength and extra pounds.

As Jimmy started to walk off the court, I hesitated and then asked, "Wanna keep playing, or do some drills?" I always wanted more, especially after taking a loss.

Jimmy seemed a little amused. "Naw, dude, I gotta roll. The guys and me are going to the football game. They're picking me up in an hour. We're gonna destroy Lincoln High tonight! Hey, you can come with us if you want."

This was a tempting offer. Here it was, only the middle of November, and I had a chance to hang out with sophomores who normally wouldn't associate with a lowly freshman. Still, I turned him down in favor of some extra practice.

"Um, thanks, it sounds cool, but I kinda need to get a little more work in."

"I should have guessed." Jimmy shook his head, "Man, I've never seen anyone play as much tennis as you. I always see you hanging out here. Does it really mean that much to you?"

"Yep." I picked up my racket and waved it in the motion of my forehand. "I may not have your athletic ability, but I'm still gonna try to compete for the top spot on the team." I joked, "The word around school is that the number one player is a real flake with crazy hair."

Jimmy smiled, "Well, freshman, it seems like you're catching on pretty quick." Flipping his hat off, he turned it around, putting it on backwards. He casually said, "Maybe that's why Kim Coleman asked about you. Man, you're lucky. She is so hot."

I nearly jumped out of my skin. "Kim Coleman asked

about me?"

Jimmy burst into laughter, "Yeah right, and the weather report says, 'cloudy skies tonight, then look for hell to freeze over!'"

I grinned sheepishly and admitted, "You got me. I guess I do have a few things to learn."

"It's cool. Just stick with *the man* and it'll be all good." Jimmy comically raised his arms and adopted the swaggering stance of a boxing champion, "I'm the king of Courage High!"

"Jimmy," I chuckled, "you've got problems."

"Hey, you really do catch on quick!" Jimmy grabbed his tennis bag and his racket. "I'm out, Bryan. See you at school tomorrow."

"All right, Jimmy, thanks for playing."

After getting a drink from the water fountain outside the court, I sat down and thought about the match. My performance had been downright terrible and I was extremely unhappy about it. It wasn't much of a consolation that Jimmy was an older and more experienced player—the bottom line was that I simply didn't get the job done out there.

On a brighter note, I felt good about having a friend as cool as Jimmy. Socially, things never came that easily for me. I guess you could say that I was pretty shy. This was my first year of high school and I was trying hard to fit in. I began to wish that I had accepted Jimmy's offer and gone to the football game with the guys. Instead, I grabbed a bucket of balls and practiced my serve.

Later that night, I lay in bed unable to sleep. The severe thrashing I had taken from Jimmy was still fresh in my mind and I just couldn't shrug it off. *I should have gone to the net more. My serve was awful.* Images of the match raced through my head like I was watching it on television. This wasn't unusual, though, because nothing—absolutely nothing—was more important to me than tennis.

I lived in a very small town in Kansas, where dreams of becoming a professional tennis player at times seemed beyond reach. I was ranked twenty-third in my state in the fourteen-and-under division, but I knew that this wasn't a particularly meaningful statistic—Kansas wasn't among the powerhouses that traditionally dominated junior tennis in the United States. In many other states I wouldn't even be ranked in the top hundred.

I sat up and leaned against my pillow, wondering if I actually had a chance to succeed in one of the most competitive sports in the world. Although I sometimes had my doubts, I was certain of one thing—*nobody* wanted it more than me. So even if the best juniors were training in places like Florida or California, I was determined that Bryan Berry, of Courage, Kansas, would find a way somehow. Maybe my town was so small that it only had one movie theater, but still, it was my home and I had no complaints. Anything would have been an improvement over those years in Wichita, before the divorce. I had been too young to understand what was going on, but it was impossible to forget the loud arguments, the slamming doors, and a hundred images of Mom crying.

Happily, the struggles of those earlier years gave way to better times, especially after our move to Courage. It was tough living two hundred miles away from Dad, but my younger brother, Brandon, and I took to small-town life immediately. We adjusted to our new schools, making friends quickly and getting involved in lots of activities. It was around that time when I went rummaging through a box of Dad's old stuff and found a tennis racket and a can of used balls. After spending a few hours hitting those yellow balls against our garage door, I was hooked. Discovering tennis changed my life forever.

Tennis had always been popular in Courage, prompting the construction of a public club twelve years earlier. It was named The Courage Courts and Recreation Club but was known to everyone simply as "The Courts." With six tennis courts, a gym, and a pool, this indoor facility had become very popular. I had practically lived there for the past three years. I went to The Courts every day after school and stayed until I had to be home for dinner. On weekends, if I wasn't entered in a tournament, I could be found there most of the day.

In between matches, I spent my time in the lounge area, watching TV, doing my homework, or sometimes just listening to the men chat. Whether the subject was sports, politics, or the latest gossip, the discussions were usually loud and very colorful. I chuckled softly as the image of a funny old-timer named Henry Johnson suddenly entered my mind. Johnson was an old man who hung out at The Courts more than I did—if that was even possible. Whenever the conversation turned to tennis, his voice always resonated loudly and passionately. He had declared many times that the champions of his era were superior to modern players. His opinions were usually met with ridicule and scorn.

"Give me a break, Henry!" The men always argued,

"Players today hit the ball harder than those old guys could have even dreamed about!"

But Johnson would stand his ground and break out some of his outlandish tennis stories, like the time that A. J. Bradford hit a serve at Wimbledon that was so fast, nobody even saw the ball as it whizzed by his opponent. According to Johnson, a big cloud of dust right on the line was the only evidence that the ball was good. Another tale recounted a doubles match in which Danny Crawford, a superstar of the 1940s, dealt with the trash-talking of an obnoxious opponent by nailing him square in the stomach with his famed topspin backhand.

Although I had doubts about whether or not his stories were true, I enjoyed hearing them. And, although I respected Johnson for his obvious love of tennis, it was easy to dismiss him as a strange old man. Apparently he had once coached a young tennis player who was on the verge of stardom when his life ended tragically. Johnny Matthews's death had such a devastating effect on Johnson that he never coached again. Instead, he'd been a teaching pro for many years, until finally retiring in Courage.

I had always accepted the fact that Johnson's knowledge of the game was totally outdated. The buzz around The Courts was that Johnson was slightly senile, maybe even crazy. I had no way of knowing if any of that stuff was true, because we had never spoken.

I leaned my head back down on my pillow, wondering why I was lying awake thinking about Henry Johnson. I certainly had more important things to worry about than a strange old man who hung around at The Courts.

CHAPTER TWO

THE COURAGE OPEN

Two months later, my alarm clock rang very early on a frigid Saturday morning in the middle of January. The Courage Open had finally arrived! Once a year, the best players in town had the opportunity to showcase their skills and challenge each other in this fiercely competitive tournament. Although I had never advanced beyond the second round, I felt good about my chances. Having celebrated my fifteenth birthday just five days earlier, I knew that I was older and stronger. Although the Courage Open didn't count for junior rankings, there was something special about playing in front of my friends and family. I hoped I could break through and make a good showing.

At 8:00 in the morning, I put on my heaviest coat and hopped onto my bike, ready to brave the bitter cold of a Kansas winter. When I arrived at The Courts, I went straight upstairs to check in at the tournament desk.

"Good morning, Bryan," said Judy Fletcher, flashing a bright smile. A true tennis aficionado, Mrs. Fletcher was working the desk for the seventh straight year, during which time she had monitored my progress with interest and enthusiasm.

"How are you, Mrs. Fletcher?" I asked politely.

"I'm always happy when the tournament rolls around. How about you?"

"I'll let you know after my match."

She laughed, "I'm sure you'll do fine. Let's see, you're playing Jeff Harris in the first round." Leaning forward, she whispered mischievously, "You know, Bryan, I'm really not supposed to favor one player over another, but if I were you, I'd play his backhand all day long."

"Thanks for the tip, Mrs. Fletcher. I'll remember that."

Now that I had checked in, there was nothing to do but wait. I knew I wouldn't have a chance to warm up because all six courts were being used for the tournament. I took a look around. The Courts had been my primary hangout for the last three years and I knew the facility inside out. The first floor consisted of the gym, pool, men and women's locker rooms, and the six tennis courts. A winding staircase led up to a huge lounge, where The Courts Grill served up tasty grub for hungry tennis players. In addition to the restaurant, the lounge had floor-to-ceiling glass windows that overlooked the courts, with couches and chairs situated so that people could watch the tennis below. On the other side of the room, there was an area with more couches, which were arranged around a big-screen

TV.

Hearing my name on the loudspeaker, I picked up my tennis bag and walked over to the desk. Judy handed me a can of balls and made the introductions, "Bryan, you know Jeff Harris, don't you?"

"Yeah, sure, how's it going?" I shook his hand nervously.

We had been assigned to court six. During our ten-minute warm-up, I took stock of my adult opponent. I smiled for a moment, realizing that Mrs. Fletcher was right about Mr. Harris's backhand. He seemed to get under it too much, resulting in a slice that floated lazily.

As the match got under way, I started out slowly, making a couple of silly unforced errors that cost me the opening game. But it didn't take me long to settle down and get things under control. After taking the first set 6-2, I was cruising at 4-1 in the second when I became a bit distracted. Looking around, I noticed that Jimmy Ellis was playing two courts away. Jimmy, who was the sixth seed, seemed to be winning easily.

My wandering concentration created an opportunity for Harris, who won a couple of games in rapid succession. I was still up a break at 4-3, but I was very upset with my lack of focus. Commanding myself to play aggressively, I won my serve with four straight points. I went on to take the match 6-2, 6-4.

When I walked back upstairs after the match, my mother, who had come to watch, greeted me. "That was good tennis, Bryan," she remarked cheerfully. "You looked terrific out there."

"Thanks, Mom. I didn't play my best, though. But as Dad likes to say, 'Any win is a good win.' Remember when he saw my match last year, how I was losing and then I came back in the second set and..." I didn't finish the sentence and suddenly became quiet. Mom understood. She was always trying to help me deal with the pain of having a father who wasn't around very much.

"He would have been proud of the way you played today, Honey," she said softly, running her fingers through my hair. We talked for a few more minutes and then discussed the plans for later. After Mom left, I walked over to the main draw, which was a large piece of cardboard that listed all the matches and scores. When I got there, I found Jimmy Ellis reviewing some of the early results. "What's up, Jimmy?"

"What's up, B?" We exchanged knuckle bumps. "What was your score?"

"Two and four," I said. "How about you?"

"Two bagels." Jimmy smiled. A bagel meant zero. Once again, Jimmy had passed through the opening round without losing a single game.

"Who do you play in the second round?" I asked.

"Second round?" Jimmy rolled his eyes. "All I know is that Kenny Singleton's gonna be waiting for me in the quarters, and he's been hitting the ball great lately."

Jimmy's confidence amazed me. He had already thrust himself into the quarterfinals. I believed that I could go that far, too, but I had none of his self-assurance. Jimmy carefully studied the draw, which was updated hourly by Judy Fletcher.

"If you win your next match, you'll probably play Ted

12

Grover in the round of sixteen. He'll drop Rick Ferguson later today." Jimmy smiled at the thought of a Berry vs. Grover match. "The all-American kid, Bryan Berry, against Ted 'The Jerk' Grover. I could sell tickets for that one! Dude, that guy will do anything it takes to win."

"Yeah, I've seen all the garbage he pulls out there, but I'm ready for it."

After we analyzed the draw for a few more minutes, Jimmy and I walked over to the large window that overlooked court number one. There, Mike Scully, the top seed in the tournament, was putting the finishing touches on a first-round slaughter. Scully, a thirty-five-year-old native of Courage and a former junior champion, was unquestionably the best player around.

The two of us stood with our noses stuck to the glass window, watching Scully crush forehand winners and effortlessly shoot aces that landed right on the lines. "Man, he's got some serious skills," I remarked.

"That's an understatement," Jimmy replied. "How many guys have ever been top ten in the nation in the eighteens when they were only sixteen?"

"Yeah, that's pretty awesome. Didn't he break into the top hundred in the world before he retired?"

"Sure did. If that back injury hadn't cut his career short, who knows how far he could have gone?"

It wasn't very long before Scully arrived at match point. His opponent could only watch helplessly as a booming first serve rocketed past and hit the backstop with a thud.

"Well, the streak continues. Five years and counting."

Jimmy was referring to the fact that Scully had steamrolled his way through the Courage Open for five consecutive years. Nobody expected this year to be any different.

Jimmy gathered up his stuff and looked at his watch. "All right, Bry, I'm gonna go home and hang out until my next match. Good luck later."

"Thanks, Jimmy, you too."

As Mike Scully casually made his way to the desk to report his scores, I stared at him with admiration. He was the greatest player I had ever watched in person. I had fantasized many times about playing him on court number one in front of everybody. The entire club would be stunned as I recorded the biggest upset in the history of the tournament.

For the time being, though, I would settle for making it past the second round. I took a look around the huge lounge, which was bustling with activity. It was much more crowded than usual because of the tournament. Several people were eating a leisurely breakfast, while others watched some of the matches in progress.

Over on the far side of the room, some of the men were milling around, talking loudly as they watched the early round tournament action. At that moment, they were engaged in a heated discussion about tennis. I could hear Old Man Johnson's sharp, clear voice exclaiming with disdain, "Oh, c'mon, look at the powerful rackets these guys use today. A little kid could wallop the ball with one of those things. In my day, the guys all used wood. When they crushed a serve you could hear the 'pop' in the cheap seats. I'll tell you this, if the players from my day had used the same rackets as these young guys today—forget about it! You wanna talk about power? In 1937, Arthur Peyton was playing the U.S. Nationals against...."

I laughed to myself—*there he goes again!* It was always fun to sit around and listen to Johnson argue with the other men, so I settled in for another lively edition of "past vs. present." By the time I checked in for my second-round match several hours later, a glance at the draw revealed that all eight seeds had advanced without dropping a single set. The tournament had a field of sixty-four, so there were two rounds today and two tomorrow. The semifinals and finals would be played next weekend.

My next opponent, Randy Kaplan, was a serve-and-volley player who attacked at every opportunity. I would have to play confident, error-free tennis to get past this match. I knew I'd have to keep my aggressive opponent back on the baseline as much as possible.

When the match began, I held serve and then hit a couple of great backhand passing shots to gain an early break. My two-handed backhand was my big weapon, a stroke that had always come naturally to me. By contrast, my forehand was much flatter and often erratic in tough situations.

Executing my game plan flawlessly, I was in control as I took the first set 6-3. But suddenly, without warning, my serve broke down and my game fell apart. Kaplan started chipping my cream puff second serve and coming in, igniting a streak that helped him seize the second set, 6-1. Everything was going wrong for me, and to my chagrin, I soon found myself down a break in the third set. The momentum clearly favored Kaplan as he moved out to a four-games-to-three lead.

At 30-all, Kaplan took a big cut at his first serve but missed long. After adjusting his racket strings, he tossed the ball up and swung at his second serve. The combination of a low toss and some bad luck led to the ball catching the top of the net and falling back onto Kaplan's side. This was a huge double fault that set up a break point for me. Kaplan stood still for an instant, as though he couldn't believe what had just happened. His flustered look gave me a jolt of confidence.

Now, at 30-40, Kaplan tried to bully his way to the net, but there wasn't much action on his serve. I pounced on it, belting a dipping topspin return with my two-handed backhand. Kaplan couldn't get there in time to catch it on the fly, leaving him with no choice but to attempt a very difficult half-volley. He got his racket on it and almost made the shot of his life. But, to his dismay, the ball once again caught the tape and rolled back to his own side.

Kaplan seemed devastated. Although the match was still dead even, 4-all in the third, it appeared as though he was re-playing those two points in his mind over and over again. A more accomplished player might have been able to fight through a run of bad luck, but Kaplan was unable to regain his compo-sure as the match slipped away from him, 7-5 in the third set.

As we shook hands at the net, I tried to be gracious in victory, "That was terrible luck on that half-volley. It should have gone over."

I accepted congratulations from my mom and Brandon, but realized that I had been lucky to survive this match. I was disappointed and began to question myself: *I'm fifteen years old, a tournament player—how am I still struggling with Randy*

Kaplan? Have I stopped improving? Is this as good as I'm going to get?

Although I wasn't too happy with myself, I tried to remain positive. I had done my job, winning both of my matches to remain alive in the tournament. It felt good to reach the round of sixteen, even though I knew that things were about to get much tougher. As Jimmy had accurately predicted, Ted Grover had scored a mild upset by eliminating the eighth seed, Rick Ferguson, in three sets. I was going to have to battle the biggest jerk in Courage.

I was so tired that I didn't even stop to look at the draw. I went straight home and spent the evening taking it easy, trying to forget about Ted Grover. As soon as my head hit the pillow at 10:30, I was fast asleep.

CHAPTER THREE

AFRAID TO LOSE

After a light breakfast at 8:00 the next morning, I tried to relax as I read the sports section. I knew that a very real challenge lay directly ahead of me. Although there was nothing exceptional about Ted Grover's game, he had a good first serve, solid strokes, and he moved surprisingly well for a man in his forties. Those skills, coupled with his reputation for "hooking," or cheating, made him a tough guy to beat.

When I arrived at The Courts with my family, I went straight upstairs to check in. Judy Fletcher was perched at the desk, examining the schedule of matches. "Ted hasn't checked in yet, Bryan, but he's on his way. I'll probably be calling your match in about twenty minutes."

I was definitely nervous as I walked over to one of the couches by the TV and sat down. I passed the time by watching a college basketball game with Brandon, while changing the overgrip on my rackets. When I saw Ted Grover walk up the stairs and check in at the desk, my heart started to beat a little faster.

The match was finally called and I got up, feeling kind of stiff. Grover didn't even acknowledge me as we collected the balls at the desk. We walked down to court four without exchanging a single word. Judy was clearly expecting a very entertaining match, because she had put us on one of the courts that were directly visible to spectators standing in the lounge upstairs.

The first few games showed how much pressure we were both feeling, because we were totally "pushing." This was an expression that meant cautiously keeping the ball in play, often resulting in long rallies that ended with unforced errors. It was frustrating, because I really wanted this match. With a spot in the quarterfinals, I would no longer be viewed as a kid who just hung out at The Courts, but as a "player." For my opponent, the stakes were just as high. Ted Grover knew he was favored to win, an expectation he was extremely eager to live up to. Recognizing this as a tremendous opportunity to reach the quarters, he had no intention of being turned away by a fifteen-year-old kid. So the stage was set.

By the time the first set went to a tiebreaker, interested spectators had crowded around the large window upstairs. In addition to Brandon and Mom, I noticed Jimmy Ellis, and, curiously, Old Man Johnson.

In crucial situations, my serve tended to be similar to my forehand—shaky and erratic. But to my surprise, I opened up the tiebreaker by nailing a clean ace. It gave me confidence, leading to some sharp tennis as I reeled off a couple of quick points. Grover suddenly seemed unsure of himself, committing a few uncharacteristic errors that helped me capture the tiebreaker 7-3.

Way to go, Bryan! The first set was in the bag. I wondered if my opponent would get discouraged and go down without a fight. Tennis is a game that requires superior mental strength, and I was about to find out if Ted Grover's head worked as well as his big mouth. Unfortunately for me, he proved to be a seasoned veteran who knew how to deal with a difficult situation. He played a very solid second set, finally breaking my serve at 4-all to grab the lead. I was thoroughly disgusted with myself. *A double fault, a loose forehand, it's like I'm giving the set away.*

At 5-4, 30-all, Grover chipped a ball to the corner and rushed in. I got there and smacked my two-handed backhand perfectly, a scorcher right up the line.

"Out!"

I stared at my opponent in disbelief. "Mr. Grover, that ball was right on the line."

"No, it was a little long," countered Grover.

I was furious, but there wasn't too much I could do. I looked up to see who was watching from upstairs. The crowd had thinned out, but Jimmy Ellis silently gestured with his hands that the ball had been good. As angry as I was, I simply couldn't afford to let a bad call disrupt my concentration. This game was too important. I jumped all over a second serve and saved a set point, fighting my way back to deuce.

Over the course of the next few minutes, I squandered some good break opportunities, missing an easy forehand and netting a volley that I didn't step into. Eventually, Grover found himself with another set point, his third in the game. After a brief rally, he charged to the net behind a deep approach, only to be totally fooled by a topspin lob that landed on the baseline. Grover didn't even chase after it. Instead, he simply gestured "out" with one finger and walked over to the sideline. I rushed over and exclaimed, "Not again, Mr. Grover! C'mon, you know that one was good!"

"Sorry, it was close, but it barely missed." He held out his fingers to indicate an inch. "One set all."

"That—that's just an outright hook!"

I was steaming, but when Grover glared at me, I became a little nervous. He was forty-four years old, a stern-looking adult with menacing eyes. I went to grab a quick drink from the water fountain outside the court, trying to forget what had just happened. We were about to play a deciding third set and I needed to keep my focus.

By the time it got to 3-all in the third, I was experiencing a case of shaky nerves. I was cautiously spinning in my serve, instead of reaching back for the power I had displayed earlier in the match. I guess that my fear of untimely double faults was causing me to play too conservatively. Sensing an opportunity, Grover started aggressively chipping my serve and coming to the net.

This game was the turning point of the match. Grover's pressure caused me to toss up a weak lob, followed by a couple of jittery forehands. Finally, at 15-40, I sealed my own fate with a double fault. As we switched sides Grover stared right at me, growling under his breath, "No punk kid is gonna stop me from getting to the quarters." He clearly intended for me to hear, and I quickly looked away as my face turned a deep red. I was ashamed that I had allowed myself to be intimidated by Grover's tactics.

Determined to storm back and win the match, I told myself to hang tough and play solid tennis. But I had lost all confidence in my forehand, and a crafty Ted Grover was making a conscious effort to keep the ball away from my potent backhand. His strategy paid off. Fifteen minutes later Grover punched a volley into the open court on match point, jubilantly raising his fist in triumph. I dejectedly gathered up my stuff and trudged up the stairs, where I was greeted with a quick hug and words of consolation from my mother.

Jimmy Ellis patted me on the shoulder, "You were robbed, dude."

Although a few spectators told me that I'd played a fine match, I felt totally demoralized. I wanted to be alone. After changing my shirt in the locker room, I wandered into the gym and sat down on one of the benches at the far end. Replaying the match in my mind, I tried to figure out what had gone wrong. But I was unable to come up with any answers. It was depressing to realize that my game was falling far short of my expectations.

I'd been lost in thought for about a half-hour when I heard the sound of approaching footsteps. I looked up and, to my surprise, Old Man Johnson was standing just a few feet in front of me. I glumly stared at the ground as he took a seat next to me.

"When the match is on the line, that's no time to play scared," Johnson drawled, as though we were old friends continuing a recent conversation. "That's the time to step up and put some pressure on your opponent, show him that you're not gonna fold."

I defended myself meekly, "Yeah, but I...I was nervous. I didn't want to start missing shots and lose the match."

"Well, that strategy didn't work. You lost anyway, right?"

"I guess so, but at the time—" My feeble search for a reasonable explanation was quickly interrupted.

"It doesn't even matter. I just wanted to come over here and tell you something. Something that I used to say a long, long time ago." There was something about Johnson's speech that captivated me. I didn't know if it was the tone of his voice, the intensity in his eyes, or the expression on his face. But I did know that every word that came out of his mouth was echoing through my head like a hurricane. "Bryan, I used to tell promising young juniors the most important words a tennis player can ever hear." He paused for emphasis, before removing his glasses and saying, "If you're afraid to lose, you can't win." And with this comment still hanging in the air, Johnson patted me on the shoulder and walked away.

Three days later I was on court four, warming up for my weekly match with Nick Armstrong, my old gym teacher from elementary school. *If you're afraid to lose, you can't win.* It felt like there was a bright neon sign in my head flashing those words over and over again. As we were hitting the ball back and forth, I was having trouble concentrating, because I was still contemplating my dismal performance in the third set of the Grover match. My inability to handle pressure had cost me a trip to the quarterfinals of my favorite tournament. The more I thought about it, the more frustrated I became. *How many more opportunities are you going to let slip away?* It took me a moment to realize that I had punctuated this thought by clubbing a ball so hard that it hit the backstop wildly. I sheepishly held up a hand to Mr. Armstrong, "Sorry."

After we had concluded our warm-ups, I prepared to serve. Just before I tossed the ball into the air, I noticed out of the corner of my eye that Old Man Johnson was watching me from the window upstairs. I threw the ball high into the air and swung mightily. Boom! A searing ace right down the center. I looked up again to see if Mr. Johnson was still there. Yep. Suddenly, I was playing inspired tennis, hitting the ball sharply and with confidence.

As soon as I applied the finishing touches to an impressive 6-2, 6-1 romp, I felt compelled to run upstairs and approach Johnson. I found him sitting at a table for two, looking as if he'd been expecting me. I sat down across from him.

"Is that what you meant by not being afraid to lose?" I asked.

"Yes," Mr. Johnson said with a wry expression as he bit into an apple, "but regrettably, the Courage Open wasn't today. You should have played like that against Grover."

I chuckled, "Yeah, you're right. I choked. Of course, Grover did steal the second set with a couple of terrible calls."

"What? Ted Grover was cheating?" Mr. Johnson's

feigned disbelief made me laugh out loud. "Believe me, Bryan, I know what he did. He's famous around here for that kind of nonsense. Still, the fact remains that your game broke down in that third set. It's too bad, because you did some good things in the match, especially in that first set tiebreaker." Everything that came out of Mr. Johnson's mouth made perfect sense to me and I began to wonder why everyone thought the old man had lost it.

"That was some of the best tennis I'd played in a long time," I said solemnly. I tried to sound more cheerful as I said, "Oh well, at least I have something to build on. I have to start somewhere."

"Yes, you do." He took another bite of his apple. "But you're going about it all wrong."

"What do you mean?" I leaned in closer.

"Well, you obviously work very hard. That's the most important thing. But unfortunately, it's not enough." He took off his old-fashioned eyeglasses. "The only thing that matters is that you develop proper technique and fundamentals. If you want to take your game to the next level, you're gonna have to start from scratch with some of your strokes."

"From scratch?" I contemplated this thought. "But won't I start losing all the time?" I asked.

"You might—at first." He took the last bite of his apple, tossing the core into a nearby garbage can. "All you juniors are too focused on trying to win. You forget that you're still learning the game. You have to develop your strokes and overcome your weaknesses, but it's impossible if all you care about is winning. Trust me, kid, if you don't fix the flaws in your game, they'll come back to haunt you one day, especially when you're faced with higher-level competition."

This observation was alarming but made a lot of sense. "I guess I've never thought about it like that. I've always tried to work hard and just get a lot of matches under my belt."

"Bryan," Johnson said gently, "I've been around the game long enough to recognize a kid who isn't progressing the way he should. When I saw you play Grover, it was clear to me that you have some problems that have never been corrected. They're not gonna just go away." I looked a little dejected. He continued, "But what was also clear to me was your instinct and ability on the tennis court. The way you move around out there is so natural, you can't teach that stuff." He leaned back in his chair. "Watching you play reminds me of someone I used to coach a long time ago."

I didn't know what he was talking about. He stared at the wall behind me blankly for a few seconds and I interrupted his thoughts, "I take it you don't care that I'm ranked twenty-third in Kansas in the fourteens."

Mr. Johnson smiled. "Believe me, kid, I would be saying the same thing even if you were number one. There are thousands of talented juniors all over America and the world who are working on their games every single day. It's them you want to compete against, not just the kids at Courage High or the kids in Kansas. Isn't that right?"

I shifted uncomfortably in my chair. How had this old man picked up on how I felt with such amazing accuracy and insight? "Yes, Mr. Johnson, you're right," I sighed. "I know I need help. What would it take to get my game on track?"

"Sacrifice, commitment, lots of hard work. And that's just for starters." He rose out of his chair and gathered his things. He was short and wiry—about five-feet-seven, 130 pounds at best. His silver hair was accented by a pair of bushy eyebrows that jumped around his forehead every time he opened his mouth to speak. After examining his wrinkled face, I estimated that he was about seventy-five years old.

"Well, I've got to be going. Promised the missus I'd be home by five o'clock today. But if you ever want to get out on the court and spend a few minutes doing some boring drills, I'd be happy to join you." He turned to leave.

"Wait a minute." I hesitated for just a split second. "How about tomorrow?" What was I getting myself into here?

Mr. Johnson looked surprised that I was taking him up on his offer. "Tomorrow?" He paused. "Tomorrow will be fine. I'll meet you here at three-thirty."

"Thanks a lot, I really appre—" But the old man was already halfway down the stairs.

When he escaped from view, I contemplated the sheer insanity of asking an old-timer like Henry Johnson for help. *Everyone at the club thinks he's totally out of it. There must be something to that.* His glasses looked like they were borrowed from Benjamin Franklin, his tennis racket looked like it came straight out of a museum, and all he talked about was the old days. But still, something about Old Man Johnson intrigued me. I wondered, *could he possibly help me become a better tennis player?* It was a long shot, a total long shot.

CHAPTER FOUR

COACH

The next day seemed to last forever. When the bell finally rang after sixth period I jumped onto my bike and raced home. Grabbing a banana from the kitchen, I went upstairs to change into my tennis clothes. Once again, the doubts that had been in my mind all day began to resurface. I thought about what Jimmy had said at school earlier, "Henry Johnson is one *strange* old dude."

For a moment I considered calling Johnson and making up an excuse about why I couldn't get together today. But I'd made a commitment and I knew I was stuck with it, so I threw my rackets in my tennis bag and trudged over to The Courts. I arrived to find Johnson sitting at a table upstairs reading the newspaper. It was quiet, which was normal for this hour of the day.

"How's it going, Mr. Johnson?"

"Fine, kid. Ready?"

"I sure am," I answered, trying to sound casual. "What court are we on?"

"We're on six, but have a seat, let's talk for a couple of minutes first."

Johnson placed the newspaper on the table and sat back. His attire consisted of a brown warm-up suit and a floppy white hat. His tennis racket, an outdated wood model, and a huge ball hopper filled with tennis balls, were on the floor next to him.

"Bryan, what are your goals in tennis over the next couple of years?"

His question caught me off guard. "Well, I need to improve and get good enough to be invited to play national tournaments. That's how I would know that I have a shot to maybe become a great player one day. Besides, having the chance to mix it up with the best juniors in the country at a tournament like Kalamazoo would be a dream come true." Kalamazoo was the most prestigious tournament in junior tennis. Getting there and playing well would signal my arrival on the national tennis scene.

"That's a noble goal. But let me tell you something, kid: it's a long, long way from Courage to Kalamazoo. Do you understand what I mean?" I nodded. "Okay, good. So let me explain why you need to get back to the basics of tennis if you ever hope to reach Kalamazoo. You see, a tennis stroke is like a computer, in the sense that it will only perform efficiently if it's programmed correctly. Your match with Grover is a perfect example. Over three long sets your backhand was great, but both your serve and forehand totally let you down. What makes one stroke so much better than another? It's not very complicated. Your backhand is programmed correctly in your computer, but your other strokes are not." The old man paused as the waitress came by and refilled his cup of coffee. "Thanks, Millie. Bryan, I don't like the way you practice because you spend all your time reinforcing bad technique—instead of learning the right way to do things. That's why your game falls apart in tough matches. Kid, you're gonna have to develop solid fundamentals, then hit so many balls that eventually your computer will replace the old program with a new one."

"I wouldn't even know where to start," I said.

"Well," Mr. Johnson said quietly, "I'm from the old school, so let's do it the old-fashioned way—let's get out there and work hard."

So that's what we did. Mr. Johnson brought the large basket of balls out on the court and stood at the net, instructing me to turn the grip on my racket to the right to create what was called a "semi-western" grip. For the next two hours, the old man fed me forehand after forehand, explaining how to get under the ball and loop it across the net to create topspin. This was a major departure for me, and I was discouraged with my inability to hit consistently. When we were done, I was bathed in sweat.

"That was terrible! I couldn't keep the ball in the court."

"Doesn't matter, Bryan. It was a good start. Let's say that you hit about twenty or thirty percent of the balls correctly. The next time, you'll try to increase that number. The goal is to be close to one hundred percent. That's when your computer will be reprogrammed. You're not gonna do it all in one day."

That night I had trouble sleeping as the events of the day swirled around in my mind. I had to admit that it had been a very rewarding experience. We had arranged to meet again the next day and I found myself impatiently looking forward to it.

Recounting the session at dinner earlier that evening, my enthusiasm had been met with skepticism.

"How can he play with you?" Mom had asked. "He's an old man, Bryan, he must be close to eighty. He can barely move around the court."

I explained that we didn't play, that the old man just fed me balls and we worked on my game. "He has a lot of cool ideas and I think he can help me. All I've been trying to do is win matches, but Mr. Johnson showed me *how* to play."

Mr. Johnson and I continued to work together every day for the next week, when I found myself matched up once again with Jimmy Ellis. The contest produced some excellent points, but also a multitude of errors—mainly from me. The last game of the match typified my erratic performance. Jimmy was serving, up a set and 5-2 in the second. I played three solid points to put him in a hole, love-40. But the changes that Mr. Johnson had instituted were causing me to play some very unpredictable tennis, and I quickly surrendered my three hard-earned break chances. Soon Jimmy arrived at match point and he kicked a serve out wide, pulling me off the court. I managed to stick out my racket and punch the ball back, setting off an intense baseline rally. Utilizing the topspin forehand that Mr. Johnson had taught me, I hit a well-placed shot deep in the court, followed by a stinging backhand that forced Jimmy out of position. He could only respond with a weak backhand that floated lazily through the air, just begging to be smacked for an easy winner. But in my haste to switch my grip over to the style that Mr. Johnson favored, I got confused and ended up being stuck with my old grip. This put the racket at an angle that wasn't favorable to hitting with topspin, and all I could muster was a woeful shot that caught the frame of my racket, landing very short on Jimmy's side. The talented lefty did the rest. With the greatest of ease, he measured a forehand and belted it well out of my reach, ending the point, and the match.

After Jimmy and I gathered our tennis bags and the used tennis balls, we walked upstairs to the lounge and ordered smoothies. As we sat down with our drinks, I told Jimmy that I had been working with Mr. Johnson for the past week.

"So I hear," Jimmy responded with a smile. "My dad told me that he's seen you here with the old man almost every day. Dude, I know you have some major psychological problems, but you're not *that* crazy, are you?"

"Don't be so sure, Jimmy," I laughed. "Seriously, though, the guy knows the game a lot better than anyone gives him credit for."

"That's kind of hard to imagine. But I guess you would know, now that you and Gramps are such good pals."

"Maybe you should come and work out with us one time. You might learn something."

Jimmy threw his arms up in mock indignation, "Learn

something? And ruin my perfect record?" His expression turned more serious. "Bryan, you should be careful. You've been with the old man for a week, and all of a sudden you're spraying the ball all over the place."

This comment got me thinking. "Yeah, I guess this whole thing does seem a little strange. Who knows, maybe I'll come to my senses eventually."

"I doubt it," Jimmy said with a grin as he got up to leave.

I picked up my drink and went to look for Mr. Johnson. Walking into the gym, I found the old man trying unsuccessfully to program a treadmill. "I'll tell you, Bryan, I'm not sure I believe in all this modern stuff. In my day we had none of these machines, but the best players could still play five sets in hundred-degree heat. So what's the point of it?"

Smiling, I replied, "Well, it's great for strength and conditioning. All you have to do is look at how good tennis players are these days. I mean, c'mon, you don't *really* think that one of those players from the old days could hang today, do you?"

In the short time we had been together, I had learned that it was impossible to win an argument with Mr. Johnson— but it was fun to try. "You don't think the old-timers could be better? Let me ask you a question, Bryan. Was there ever a better hitter than Babe Ruth? Was there ever a better athlete than Jesse Owens? And was there ever a better singer than the legendary Caruso?"

I laughed heartily. *Who the heck was Caruso?* At that moment I was struck by how comfortable I felt when I was around Mr. Johnson, and how much he made me believe that I could actually accomplish something in tennis. Nobody had ever made me feel like that before. Suddenly, without thinking, I blurted out, "Will you be my coach?"

Mr. Johnson stared at me for what seemed like an eternity. "Are you sure that's what you want? Because a lot of people would say that you're making a mistake."

He was right. I was a ranked junior who had been taking lessons from legitimate teaching pros for several years. There was no question that I had improved. To switch over to Henry Johnson seemed utterly ridiculous and a huge gamble. Even though the old man had been a teaching pro in his younger days, his credentials were not exactly dazzling. His only claim to fame was that he had once coached a well-known junior, the one who died, but that was over fifty years ago.

But the bottom line was that I had big-time dreams in tennis and, regardless of what anyone else might think, I had come to the conclusion that this grizzled old man could help me get there. He had coached that kid, Johnny Matthews, to the very brink of stardom. Could there be enough magic left in his old bones to do it again?

"You with me, kid?" Mr. Johnson tried to jolt me from my daydream.

"Yes, sir." Our eyes met and I said, "There's nothing in the world I want more than to become a great tennis player. Can you help me?"

As if deep in thought, he looked past me and onto the tennis courts. A few seconds later he extended his hand and I shook it. "I think I can, Bryan. Be here tomorrow at three-thirty and we'll get started. We've got a lot of work to do."

The next day I showed up at The Courts with a slight swagger and a smile on my face. I had a new coach! But by the time I wearily dragged myself home that evening, the swagger was long gone. I thought of the old proverb, *"Be careful what you wish for, it may come true."* I definitely wanted to work hard, but I hadn't been prepared for three punishing hours of running, hitting, and drilling. And this was only a preview of things to come. Mr. Johnson and I started getting together four or five times a week. Each session was challenging and strenuous, as he tried to correct various flaws in the mechanics of my strokes. He constantly reminded me to bend my knees, get under the ball, or follow through on a shot. When I tired, the old man urged me on, encouraging me to find the strength to keep trying.

During moments of rest, or when we were off the court, Mr. Johnson and I would talk about the finer points of tennis. "Let me ask you a question, kid. When you attack the net, how do you decide whether you should protect the line or cover the crosscourt?"

"I'd say instinct and anticipation."

"Yes, I agree. But there's more to it than just that. Let's say you're in a match and the guy is going crosscourt something like seven out of every ten times. On a big point, what's the percentage play?"

"Cover the crosscourt."

"Very good, Einstein. That's not to say he won't hit it up the line and win the point. But more often than not, a guy will go with his strength, especially if it's an important situation. So you want to be aware of what that strength is."

"I never really thought about tennis like that."

"Some athletes always look for an edge, Bryan, and I want you to learn from them. If you keep your eyes open during the course of a match, you just might notice something that could help you on a key point."

Each meeting with my new mentor was a journey into uncharted territory as we explored aspects of tennis that I had never even considered. Mr. Johnson always allotted the first couple of hours for the forehand and serve, two shots he was overhauling from top to bottom. Then we would choose one or two different strokes and drill them endlessly. Whether it was the drop shot, the drop volley, the approach shot, or anything else, we were sure to practice it.

The conclusion of every session was always devoted to several conditioning drills, including a brutal "game" that entailed nonstop corner-to-corner running. I always tried to give one hundred percent no matter how tired I felt. But the day would still not be complete. We would walk into the gym, where Mr. Johnson would put me through a lengthy "old-school" program of jumping rope, push-ups, sit-ups, and jumping jacks.

These marathon workouts left me more exhausted than I had ever imagined possible. But it was exciting to train at a higher level, especially with someone by my side who was just as enthusiastic and ambitious as I was. Mr. Johnson's passion for tennis was inspiring.

Not surprisingly, I was taking some heat from some of the adults at The Courts about my new coach. Although most of it was good-natured kidding, it was sprinkled with the implication that I was making a grave mistake. Apparently, nothing could alter the perception that Henry Johnson was a crazy old man living in a world that had long since passed him by.

It would have been nice to dispel that notion by winning some tennis matches, but unfortunately the exact opposite was happening. Now that I had moved from the fourteen-and-under division up to the sixteens, I was finding it difficult to win matches in junior tournaments. I still hadn't taken a set from Jimmy Ellis, and I also suffered a few "bad" losses to people I was accustomed to beating.

I understood why I was having problems on the court. My new serve had no consistency, leading to double faults at the most inopportune times. Even more costly, though, was the process of learning an entirely new grip on my forehand. During matches, there were numerous times when I would get caught with the wrong grip, resulting in an errant shot.

So in spite of the fact that I hit the ball well in the practice sessions, I was losing to everybody. I expressed my frustration to Mr. Johnson, lamenting that it sometimes felt like it would never come together. The old man was quick with a reassuring response, "Bryan, everyone knows the cliché 'no pain, no gain,' right?" I nodded. "Well, this is a version of it. I've never understood why people are unwilling to sacrifice some wins in order to make their games better in the long run. It's frustrating, but unfortunately it's the only way. I believe that it takes at least six months to properly retool a stroke. And during that time, there will be days that you can't seem to hit the ball over the net."

"You can say that again."

Mr. Johnson laughed. "Yeah, I know, you've had some rough outings. But trust me, kid, one day you'll be rewarded for all the pain and suffering you're enduring. Once your new strokes are permanently programmed in your computer, you'll be a totally different player."

"But I guess there's still a long road ahead of us."

"I'm afraid so, kid. These things don't just happen overnight. But when everything finally falls into place, it will be the greatest feeling in the world."

CHAPTER FIVE

DAD'S BACK

"Hey Dad."

"Hi Champ! How's it going?" My dad got up from the couch, where he had been playfully wrestling with my brother, to give me a big bear hug. He lifted me into the air and I couldn't help but smile.

I had just come home from school on a sunny day in late March, and when I saw Dad's car parked in my driveway, I wasn't shocked. Every once in a while Dad would show up unexpectedly to spend a couple of whirlwind days with Brandon and me, only to disappear just as quickly. Brandon was twelve years old, still young enough to be forgiving, but I felt deep pain because my dad never seemed to be around when I really needed him.

"I hear you're hitting the cover off the tennis ball these

days, Champ. Maybe you'll give your old man a chance to see you play."

I thought about all the times I'd given him that chance, only to be blown off or forgotten about. "Yeah, sure," I said quietly. "I'd like that."

Mom was sitting on the couch keeping an eye on everything, and I was pretty sure that she understood why my reaction to my father's appearance was so subdued. I had confided in her that these random visits always seemed to inspire hope that inevitably ended in disappointment for me.

"How long are you in town for, Paul?" she asked.

"I'm not sure, but we'll have fun while I'm here, right, boys?"

"Right!" exclaimed Brandon. His enthusiasm was beginning to rub off on me. Even though I was trying hard to play it cool, I loved my dad and was happy to see him.

Dad stood tall in front of us and spoke in a serious voice, "I have an announcement to make and I guess that now is as good a time as any to make it." He avoided my mother's eyes when he said, "I've been seeing someone for quite some time now and, well, we were in Las Vegas last week, and it was a spur-of-the-moment thing, but...I guess what I'm trying to say is that I got married."

A new record for my dad! Only five minutes in town and he'd already thrown us a big-time curveball. I glanced sideways at my mother and our eyes met briefly. Her face was solemn and rigid but she remained silent.

"Her name is Lisa," Dad continued, "and she's here in Courage with me. We're staying over at the motel, but I just thought I'd come over first and tell you the news."

I was at a loss for words. Although I wasn't entirely surprised, I knew that this development erased any faint hope that my parents might someday get back together.

"Kathleen, if it's okay with you I'd like to take the guys to dinner so they can have a chance to meet Lisa."

"Of course." It wasn't hard to detect a trace of sarcasm in Mom's voice. "Boys, go put on something decent."

Brandon and I raced upstairs, leaving our parents sitting together in uncomfortable silence. I was getting dressed when I heard my dad finally say, "You've done a good job with them, Kathleen. They're great kids."

"I know they are. They have pretty much everything they need—except for a relationship with their father. That's what they really want."

"I know, Kathleen. I admit that I haven't been much of a father, but I'm going to change all that."

"I've heard that before." Mom started to walk into the kitchen.

Dad's voice got a little sharper, "Look, there's nothing I can do about the past. But I've stopped drinking, I'm happy for the first time in years, and—" Dad paused when he noticed Brandon and me standing at the foot of the stairs. We knew from experience that we could usually break up one of their arguments by simply appearing.

"That was quick," Dad said, rising out of his chair. He forced a smile and said, "I'll have them home early, Kathleen. All right, guys, let's go!"

Kissing our mom on the way out, Brandon and I cheerfully argued about what restaurant we wanted to go to. We weren't going to let our parents' bickering spoil the joy of being with our dad. And although I had decided in advance that I probably wasn't going to like Lisa, her beaming smile won me over quickly. Although I had always fantasized about a reunion between my parents, I had to admit that my father truly seemed to be happy with her.

As a memorable week of sports, movies, and pizza flew by, it was obvious that my dad and Lisa enjoyed hanging out with us. Sitting in a restaurant on our last night together, I dreaded the answer to the question that had been on my mind all week, "Dad, when will you and Lisa visit again?"

"Yeah," Brandon chimed in, "every time you leave, it's like *years* until you come back." Everyone laughed, but I was glad that the subject was out in the open.

"Well, guys, funny you should mention that, because it's not going to be years. As a matter of fact, I'm going to be back here in a week."

"A week?" Something was up, because that didn't sound like my dad at all.

"And that's not all. Lisa and I have some news for you." Dad paused for effect.

"C'mon, Paul, don't keep the boys in suspense," Lisa said, tapping him on the shoulder.

"Okay, drum roll please." Dad loudly created his own sound effect and then said, "What do you guys think about California?"

I had a feeling I knew where this was heading. Dad was moving to California, which was like a million miles from

Kansas. Now I'd really never see him. "Where in California, Dad?" I asked in an annoyed voice.

"Los Angeles."

"Wow, *Los Angeles*," Brandon whistled softly. "Sunny days, beaches, and movie stars."

Dad and Lisa smiled, and then Dad looked me right in the eye, "Here's the situation. I got offered a job out there and it's just too good to pass up. So Lisa and I are moving and it's gonna be fantastic, but there's one thing that would make it absolutely perfect—if you guys were living with us out there."

"What?" He said it so casually that he caught me off guard. "Move to California? What about Mom?" I asked.

"Well, as you might imagine, your mother isn't very receptive to the idea, but I told her to consider what would be best for you guys. Don't forget Bryan, Los Angeles is the home of some of the most excellent junior tennis players in the country. And Brandon, we're only a five-minute drive from the beach! Anyway, your mother and I are going to talk to a judge about it next Friday."

"Oh," I said quietly, as something connected in my mind. I had seen my mom looking over official-looking documents for the past few days, but she had refused to talk about them with me. Now I understood why.

Later that night, after Dad dropped us off, I tried to press Mom for more information. She still didn't want to talk about it and she seemed very annoyed that my dad had even mentioned it. I could see that she was trying to play it off to me like it was nothing major, but I felt certain that she was scared of losing us.

Although we all tried to carry on like nothing was out of the ordinary, there was a noticeable degree of tension in the air for the next couple of days as Mom prepared for her court appearance. When the day finally arrived, I was nervous thinking about it while I was at school. Was something going to happen that would shake up the rest of my life? Throughout the day, I kept trying to envision what was happening in court and what the judge was saying.

The proceeding must have taken longer than expected, because when I got home Brandon was there with Ella, the housekeeper who came on Tuesdays and Fridays and left when Mom got home. I walked into the kitchen, poured myself a glass of milk and made an extra-thick turkey sandwich. Grabbing the latest edition of *Tennis Monthly*, I sat down at the table with my food and started flipping through the magazine. I could feel Brandon's eyes upon me.

"Bryan, why is it taking so long?"

"I don't know, Brandon. It's not that complicated. After Mom and Dad each take their best shot at telling the judge why we would be better off living with them, he makes a final decision and that's the end of it."

Brandon hesitated. "What if the judge tells us to move to Los Angeles with Dad?"

Although that scenario had been running through my mind all day, I tried to act very knowledgeable and confident. "That's not gonna happen. A judge doesn't just say, 'okay kids, you're moving.' There has to be a reason and I can't think of one. And anyway, c'mon Brandon, Dad comes around every once in a while and does his father-of-the-year routine, and then he bails. Now all of a sudden he wants us to leave our home and our friends? I'm not feelin' that at all."

"I don't want to leave either, but aren't you curious about what it would be like to live with Dad?"

"Well, maybe a little," I admitted. Actually, it was more than a little. I had spent much of the day sitting in class daydreaming about California. I pictured myself playing tennis with the warm sun on my back, and then taking a dip in the cool ocean. I also thought a lot about my dad. But instead of feeling excitement about the prospect of being with him every day, I actually felt scared. I didn't want to leave Mom. She had always been there for me and I knew that would never change. Dad, on the other hand, was about as consistent as my forehand. I confided some of my true feelings to Brandon, "Why would I want to leave everything I love here in Courage to live with a guy who spent the last fifteen years avoiding me? I just wish he'd act like a real dad here in Courage, instead of trying to drag us across the country." My voice was sharp and angry.

"Man, Bryan, you're really mad," Brandon said.

He was right, I was venting my frustration about my dad not being a part of our lives on a regular basis. I guess I was a little resentful that he would try to make it up to us with some crazy plan like moving us to California. I was about to explain this to Brandon, when suddenly we heard the sound of Mom's car pulling up. Brandon and I looked at each other. For a single moment I was struck by a sense of uncertainty. What news would Mom bring? She walked in the house and tried to act nonchalant, but I could tell she was relieved by the way she hugged us tightly. "Okay, boys, don't worry, nothing is going to change. You're still stuck with me in Courage." She refused to give us any of the details.

Later that evening Brandon and I had dinner with Dad, who was planning to leave the next morning. He told us that he had expected this outcome and wasn't disappointed, but he had felt he needed to give it a try. He said that in spite of the fact that he was moving to Los Angeles over the summer, he had every intention of becoming a larger and more stable part of our lives. *I'll believe that when I see it*, I thought to myself.

I had so many jumbled feelings about my dad and I knew deep in my heart that I was going to have to deal with them eventually. But moving thousands of miles away to California would not have been the answer. Courage was the only real home I had ever known and I couldn't even imagine living anywhere else. I had a busy life here with school and my friends—and a strange old man who was my new tennis coach.

CHAPTER SIX

JOHNNY MATHEWS

On a warm Saturday in April, I was a guest at Mr. Johnson's home for an early dinner. The old man had extended me the invitation by saying, "The wife wants to meet you." So after a long and productive workout, we left The Courts together, me trailing Mr. Johnson's old car on my bike.

Mr. Johnson lived in a small, one-story house on a quiet street at the far end of Courage. The exterior could have used a paint job, but the inside was warm and inviting.

"Liz, this is the kid," was the introduction given in Mr. Johnson's matter-of-fact style.

"Bryan, it's a pleasure. I've heard so many nice things about you."

"Thank you, ma'am. I'm very glad to meet you."

Elizabeth Johnson was a pleasant-looking, white-haired

woman who appeared to be in her early seventies. Wearing a colorful dress and an apron tied around her waist, she reminded me of my own grandmother, who was living in Florida.

"You boys can relax in the living room until dinner is ready. Are you hungry, Bryan?"

I glanced at Mr. Johnson. It was clear that there was no need for formality here. "Yeah, I'm always starving after one of our workouts."

"Good," said Elizabeth, "because Henry told me to make a lot of food. Now go sit down."

I took a seat in an old leather armchair, settling back comfortably. I noticed that some framed photographs were arranged neatly on the table beside me. One was of Mr. Johnson and Elizabeth with the inscription:

Chicago, 1973

But it was another one that caught my eye, a photo of a young Mr. Johnson with two other men in tennis clothes.

"Who are these two?"

"That's me with A. J. Bradford and Danny Crawford in California in 1944."

I was surprised. "Wow, you really did know famous pros."

"Sure, I knew them all. I was teaching at the Los Angeles Tennis Club, the premier club in California at that time. That's where most of the top pros worked out when they were in town."

I touched the picture with my finger, "That must have

been so cool."

"It sure was. Those were good times, and I had the best job in the world." He smiled and said, "I had the good fortune to spend most of my time working with promising juniors just like you."

"Mr. Johnson," I said slowly, poised to ask the question I had wanted to ask for weeks now, "I—I've heard that you had a big-time junior who died." Mr. Johnson was silent for a moment, causing me to wonder if it had been a mistake to bring it up. I started to say, "I'm sorry, forget that I even—"

"It's okay, Bryan. That's true. I had a junior who was the real thing—a kid by the name of Johnny Matthews. He was a street urchin when I found him. Do you know what that means?" I shook my head. "That was an expression we used to have for a kid with no home. Johnny's father was alive, but he was a no-good drunk who couldn't take care of his own son. When Johnny was thirteen, he started hanging around the Los Angeles Tennis Club. He would sneak in at off-hours to hit balls against the wall, for hours at a time. Once I caught him sleeping in the members lounge because his dad had locked him out of his house. He was a kid who had nothing."

"When did you start working with him?"

"Soon after that, when I saw how serious he was about tennis. He had never taken a lesson in his life, but he had a beautiful natural game. He moved around the court with less effort than anyone I've ever seen." The old man paused as he got up and reached for two cans of sodas, handing one to me. Then he continued, "I worked with Johnny for over four years, between 1945 and 1949. He was absolutely destroying the jun-

51

iors in California. I would have him work out with the pros when they were in town, and he could hang with all of them. He was only seventeen at the time! All he needed was some seasoning and a couple more years of tournament experience. I had him scheduled to play a whole summer of nationals when it happened." There was another pause as Mr. Johnson took a sip of his drink.

"What happened?" I asked, leaning in closer.

"It was a Sunday in early June, back in '49. We had practiced as usual in the morning, preparing Johnny for a tournament in Santa Barbara, which was starting the next day. That night he drove out there with his doubles partner, Mark Thompson. Johnny was seeded number one in singles, and together they were the top seed in the doubles. Thompson called me up late that night. He was hysterical. He told me that he and Johnny had stopped at a roadside diner to have a bite. While they were eating, two men came in carrying guns, demanding money. Apparently, the men took a liking to one of the waitresses and decided to kidnap her. She screamed in horror, knowing what would happen if she had to go with them. When the men turned toward the exit, Johnny jumped up—so quick that nobody even moved—and he attacked both men. He decked one guy, but when he turned to the other, there was a struggle. The gun went off and Johnny died instantly." Mr. Johnson's voice dropped. "The papers said that he was a hero. They were right." I could see that his eyes were moist.

"I'm sorry I brought back all those memories," I said.

"Don't be sorry. I'm glad you did. You know, I haven't told that story for almost thirty years. I've tried to forget, but I never could. It feels good to talk about it again." Mr. Johnson patted me on the back.

"Do you have a picture of him?" I asked.

"I sure do. I'll show you after dinner, okay? And I'll bet you're ready to eat." He called out, "How's dinner coming, Liz? You've got a hungry young tennis player in here."

Elizabeth's good-natured laugh could be heard from the kitchen, "Sit right down, boys. Everything is ready."

Dinner was lively, fun, and very filling. As we ate, Mr. Johnson entertained us with stories of his youth, playing tennis, serving in the army, and meeting his bride. I asked Elizabeth how long they had been married. "Fifty-five years this July," she replied proudly.

"That's amazing," I said. "Do you have a secret?"

Elizabeth smiled, "The secret is that I never remind this old man how many times he's told each particular story of his. I pretend they're brand new every time I hear them!"

I laughed, "You know, the people at The Courts don't seem to believe a lot of your stories, Mr. Johnson."

"Yes, I know, but I've never lived my life based on what people said about me. I've made mistakes, sure, but I have no regrets. I've served my country, I've known legendary tennis players, and I was lucky enough to marry the prettiest girl in town. So those people can say or think whatever they want. I really don't care." He took one last bite and smiled, "Well I'm stuffed."

"Me too. That was an incredible dinner, Mrs. Johnson, thank you so much." I got up from the table, following Mr. Johnson into a large room that was cluttered with books and magazines. I gazed in awe at the shelves that were overflowing with trophies. There were more there than I could count. I read the inscriptions:

Winner, 1948 Los Angeles Griffith Park Boys 16 & Under, Johnny Matthews

Winner, 1949 Santa Monica Boys 18 & Under, Johnny Matthews

I continued to study the trophies one by one as Mr. Johnson, who was seated at his desk, shuffled through stacks of papers until he found what he was looking for. He handed me a newspaper clipping that was yellow and fading. On the top Mr. Johnson had written, *"Los Angeles Times, September 19, 1948."* The headline read, "The Life and Times of Johnny Matthews," and the story was printed as follows:

He came from a broken home. He used to cut classes on a regular basis. He appeared in Juvenile Court twice before his thirteenth birthday. Yet, as sixteen-year-old tennis prodigy Johnny Matthews capped off an undefeated summer by easily marching through the Southern California Sectionals last week, people were whispering that he just might be the future of American tennis.

This likeable youngster stands six-feet-two-inches tall, relying on every inch to unleash his huge cannonball serve. Coupled with fluid, elegant groundstrokes, it adds up to the total package. And don't let his dynamic personality and impish grin fool you—this kid is ferocious on the court, demolishing hapless opponents with merciless precision. When I asked Johnny how he overcame his rocky childhood and developed such a marvelous game, he said, "Three words—Coach Henry Johnson. He took me in and gave me something better to do than get in trouble. We've been working together for almost four years, and this summer it all started to pay off."

After speaking with Johnny, I caught up with Henry Johnson, who is regarded as one of the most prominent figures in California junior tennis. I asked Johnson how far Johnny could go in tennis. "The sky's the limit," he told me. "This kid is the real thing."

The rest of the article was barely legible, but I got the gist of it from what I'd read. I looked at Mr. Johnson with true remorse. This old man had surely deserved better luck from the game of tennis. Without a word, he handed me a stack of photos. The one on top was a picture of a kid in his teens standing next to a youngish Henry Johnson. They were both smiling and holding tennis rackets. In the background was the entrance to a club with a large sign that read "Los Angeles Tennis Club." Johnny was tall and thin, with tousled hair and a carefree sparkle in his eyes.

We sat on the couch looking through photographs and newspaper clippings for a few more minutes. I was lost in thought, but finally I looked over at the old man and asked, "Mr. Johnson, remember when you said I remind you a little of Johnny? Did you mean as a tennis player?"

"You bet I did. You move around the court the way Johnny used to—naturally, without effort. And you treat the game with respect and dedication, just like he did. Johnny really loved tennis, same as you."

"But my game has so many flaws."

"That may be true, Bryan, but we're going to correct them, you'll see. Everything will happen in its own time." Mr. Johnson paused, chuckling softly. "It's funny, Bryan. Johnny used to worry about his game, just like you. And I'll tell you the same thing I told him, which is to put the doubts out of your mind. I know you're concerned because you're losing to a few people, but believe me, it doesn't matter one bit. All you're doing is taking one step backward to take two forward. It'll be worth it, I promise."

A few minutes later I was hopping onto my bicycle in Mr. Johnson's front yard. "Thanks for everything, Mr. Johnson, I had a great time today. You've taught me so much already, and there's no way for me to tell you how much I appreciate it."

"That's nice of you to say, kid." The old man's voice was gruff, but the emotion could not be masked, "So let me teach you one more thing. From now on, no more 'Mr. Johnson.' Call me Henry."

"Yes sir, uh, Henry. Thanks a lot." Then I asked light-heartedly, "Did you let all your students call you Henry?"

"No," replied the old man with complete seriousness. "Only Johnny."

I smiled as I pedaled down his winding driveway toward home.

CHAPTER SEVEN

A LOONY OLD QUACK

A month later—four months after my training with Henry had begun—I played a practice match against Ted Grover. I guess I should have known it was going to be a rough day, because it certainly started off on the wrong foot. When I woke up, I read a long e-mail from Dad that put me in an emotional and slightly confused mood. He told me that he knew I was upset with him, but he wanted to find a way back into my life. He explained how he had married my mom when they were both very young and not ready for the responsibilities of married life. Before long, they had two little children, bills to pay, and he was stuck in a job that he hated. He admitted that he had made terrible choices, but he claimed that he had spent several years confronting his mistakes and growing. According to Dad, Lisa had played a major role in that process, helping him to kick his drinking habit once and for all. Now the only thing left was to reconnect with his children.

I wanted to believe everything he was saying, but I was skeptical. In the past, every time my dad had given me hope that things were changing, it would always end up being more of the same—no calls, no e-mails, no contact for extended periods of time. Mom said that I was protecting myself because I didn't want to get hurt again, but she encouraged me to write back to him and keep the lines of communication open. I didn't know what to do.

After such an unsettling beginning to the day, I was happy to get my mind off the drama and escape to The Courts for my match. But as I waited around for Grover, who arrived almost an hour late, I became agitated, even angry. Grover, arrogant as ever, got under my skin with a snide comment about my poor results over the last couple of months. I tried to stay focused and ignore his nasty words, but I was in a bad mood and totally unprepared for a difficult match.

As we began to play, I pretty much abandoned the fundamentals that Henry and I were working so hard to develop. On the very first point I tried to return Grover's serve with an outright winner, but it missed by a mile. This was a trend that continued as I simply tried to blow him off the court—a huge mistake. My ill-conceived strategy backfired, and unfortunately, everything went wrong in a disheartening 6-2, 6-2 thrashing. The bad days had been coming with less frequency recently, but this subpar performance was downright embarrassing.

I stayed on the court to hit some serves after the match, venting my frustration by forcefully walloping a couple of balls.

But I soon calmed down, knowing that Henry would dismiss the significance of this one match and remind me that we were in it for the long haul. I decided to go upstairs to wait for Henry, who was at a doctor's appointment. When I got up to the lounge, I passed by a group of men, who were eating lunch as they watched a baseball game on TV.

"So how'd you do, Bryan?" inquired Neil Avery, munching on a sandwich. He already knew the answer to this question because Ted Grover had stopped by the table a couple of minutes earlier to revel in his victory.

"He got me today," I replied graciously.

"Oh, really? What was the score?"

"Two and two."

Like most juniors, I found it distressing to report a losing score, but Henry had taught me to handle defeat with dignity. I started to walk toward the locker room but was stopped by the sound of Harry Benson's booming voice. "Two and two? You had a much closer match with him at the tournament this year. Didn't he beat you in three sets?"

"Yeah, six-three in the third."

"Hmmm," Benson uttered loudly, "maybe you're moving in the wrong direction, Bryan. You should be getting more even with him, not less."

"Well, I guess I had a bad day. Happens sometimes."

Benson glanced over at Avery, who was wiping his face with a napkin, "Neil, this doesn't sound like a case of a kid having one bad day. To me, it sounds like Ted clearly has Bryan's number. Wouldn't you agree?"

"Yep."

"As a matter of fact, Bryan hasn't been beating anybody lately, has he?"

"Not from what I've heard," replied Avery smugly.

Benson turned his attention back to me, "Let's face the facts, Bryan. You've been going straight downhill ever since you started hanging around with the old man. Maybe you should get back to taking lessons from somebody who knows what he's doing."

Two of the men offered mock applause to emphasize the point. I looked at them. Although the group had never been deliberately unfriendly toward me, they had never made me feel very much at home either. "I'm pretty comfortable with Henry, thanks. We're doing just fine together."

"I'm not trying to give you a hard time, Bryan, it's just that I'm concerned for you." Benson tried to soften his voice, but it dripped with insincerity. He was obviously enjoying himself, at my expense. "What in the world is he teaching you?"

I was starting to lose my patience, but I tried to keep my composure, reminding myself that I was the kid and they were the adults. "Oh, a lot of different stuff," I said. "Things that have proven successful for him in the past."

This time it was Avery who couldn't resist the temptation to get in on the fun, "Bryan, I hate to be the one to break it to you, but *nothing* has proven successful for him in the past."

I was on the verge of exploding, but I stopped myself, again starting to walk toward the locker room. But Benson's voice resonated loudly, "Bryan, he's a loony old quack from the 1940s and everybody knows it."

That did it. After the kind of day I was having, this

pushed me over the edge. I was upset about the situation with my dad, I had suffered a humiliating defeat to Grover, and now this attack on Henry. I looked right at him and said, "Mr. Benson, let me tell you something that will probably come as a surprise to you, since you don't realize what an obnoxious person you are: I'll bet that Henry was a lot smarter and nicer than you even when he was a young guy back in the 1940s. He definitely is today."

Benson's face grew bright red amidst a chorus of "oohs" and whistles. Rarely at a loss for words, this was one time that he was unable to muster a reply. As I quickly turned around to walk away, I suddenly noticed Henry stepping forward from the left of the staircase, where he had been standing. The old man had been there the entire time.

The group of men fell absolutely silent, leading to a couple of very long, awkward moments. As for me, however, I cracked a little smile as soon as I saw the familiar expression on the old man's face. There was no visible emotion, only an amused twinkle in his eye. Finally, Henry said loudly, "Let's go, kid. This loony old quack wants to get out on the tennis court and do a little work."

I laughed and followed Henry down the stairs, more eager than ever to work hard.

A couple of weeks later, three days before a crucially important tournament that would mark the beginning of my quest to qualify for the nationals, I was at The Courts playing a practice match against Bruce Palmer. After two hours on the court, our tightly contested battle was deadlocked at 4-all in the third set. After splitting the first six points of the game,

Palmer found the sweet spot on his racket, delivering a thunderous serve that had "ace" written all over it. But I was lucky enough to move in the correct direction and stab at the ball, punching it back over the net with just enough depth to prevent Palmer from attacking. Instead, he smoothly hit a low-slicing backhand that set off a long baseline rally. Several shots later, as I scrambled to the corner to retrieve Palmer's wide forehand, I turned quickly to get back into the court. Unfortunately, my left foot didn't turn with me. I let out a loud yell as I crumpled to the ground, clutching my ankle. Palmer immediately ran over.

"What happened? Are you hurt, Bryan?"

I was in a lot of pain. I gasped, "My ankle!"

"Take that shoe off, Bryan. Let's see how bad it is."

"No!" exclaimed a voice behind us. Henry, who had been watching from upstairs, bolted down to the court faster than he'd moved in thirty years. "Don't take that shoe off yet." Henry's voice carried a sharp ring of authority. "Let Bruce help you get up the stairs and we'll work on it there." Henry huffed and puffed as he made his way back up to the lounge.

Leaning against Palmer for support, I hopped up to the lounge and carefully lowered myself on a couch. Henry returned a minute later with two ice packs and a handful of towels. As I gently removed my sock and shoe, I was dismayed to find that my ankle had already swelled up quite a bit. Henry used the towels to prop up my foot, and then he gingerly placed the ice packs over the swollen area. He seemed very calm, as though this wasn't anything out of the ordinary. After adjusting the position of the ice packs, he sat back.

"How bad does it look?" I asked fearfully.

"Well, when the swelling goes down you can get it x-rayed, but I'm pretty sure that it's only a sprain."

"The Missouri Valley Supers Circuit tournament is this Saturday. Do you think there's a chance?"

"I'm afraid not, kid. You did this baby up right. It's gonna be a little while before you're back out on the court."

"I don't believe it! After all the work we've done to prepare for the tournament, it's gone, just like that? Oh, man, it couldn't have come at a worse time."

"I don't know about that," Henry chuckled. "Better now than at Wimbledon, right?" The thought of me playing at Wimbledon, the most prestigious professional tournament in the world, made me smile. Henry continued, "Every athlete has to deal with injuries at one point or another. All that matters is that we do everything we can to get you completely healed up. You have a lot of work to do over the summer, and the last thing we need is for this to linger."

"Yeah, you're right, this summer's much more important than a few weeks. I guess it's not even that big of a deal to miss the tournament. It was probably unrealistic anyway to think that I had a chance to qualify for the nationals this summer."

"Well, you always want to think that you have a chance, but we both know that you're not yet at the level of national players. But this is only your first year of sixteens, so you'll have another shot next year. We'll make sure you're ready by then."

The following week seemed endless. The x-ray had

come up negative, confirming Henry's diagnosis of a severe sprain. It was frustrating that I couldn't be out on the court, especially while every other tennis player in the State of Kansas was preparing for a series of crucial tournaments. But there was nothing I could do about it.

I met Henry at The Courts on a Tuesday, almost two weeks after the injury had occurred. Henry inspected the ankle closely, pronouncing that it was much better. It was. Although there was still some tenderness and pain, the swelling had subsided. I was able to start hitting the ball around very lightly, without running much. It felt strange to be back on the tennis court, but wonderful, like being reunited with an old friend. Soon I was running at full speed again, and the injury was quickly becoming a distant memory.

By the end of June, a small, select group of the best juniors across the country had qualified to participate in national tournaments. Unfortunately that opportunity had passed me by—for this summer at least—but still, I was happy and grateful to be back at full strength, hitting the ball better than ever.

CHAPTER EIGHT

SUMMER VACATION

In spite of such an unlucky beginning to the summer, things picked up quickly for me. Something special was happening out on the tennis court, where major breakthroughs seemed to be occurring on a regular basis. Under Henry's watchful eye, holes were being patched up and deficiencies were magically disappearing into thin air.

I was finally starting to switch grips automatically from forehand to backhand, with startling results. My flat, uneven forehand had vanished, replaced by a devastating topspin shot that I could hit anywhere I pleased. Sometimes it was hard to believe that it was me—Bryan Berry—hitting these powerful groundstrokes with such grace and ease. It made me hungry to work even harder.

The countless hours we had devoted to the serve were

beginning to pay off as well. Henry managed to rid me of a hitch in my swing, so that I now had a smooth, continuous motion. With that barrier removed, we worked on turning the hips, bending the knees, and extending fully to create a real snap. Although the consistency still wasn't there yet, I was starting to use my entire five-foot-ten-inch frame to crack the kind of serves I had always dreamed about.

As the summer raced on, my rigorous work with Henry was complemented by a very busy schedule of state tournaments. Obviously, the level of competition wasn't even close to national tournaments, but still, I was pleased that I was getting to the semis and finals of these events with regularity.

My success wasn't altogether surprising. With grooved strokes and dramatically improved fitness, my well-rounded game had thrust me far ahead of people who had been beating me just a year earlier. I was becoming recognized as one of the best juniors in Kansas, a distinction that spurred my confidence even more.

Ironically, when compared with Henry's demanding training sessions, the tournaments were almost a relief. The old man had taken it easy on me while I was coming back from the injury, but now the intensity of our workouts was greater than it had ever been before. So while people in Courage were enjoying the splendor of a Kansas summer, Henry and I were laboring, both outdoors as part of our training, and indoors at The Courts.

One of the highlights of my summer was an excursion to the big city with Henry to watch an exhibition match between Chris Conrad and Jake Sanders, the top two Americans in the world. I had never seen live professional tennis and I could hardly contain my excitement as Henry's old car rumbled down Interstate 135 on the way into Wichita. As Henry drove, I read aloud from an article in the sports section, which described the rivalry between the two American superstars. The opportunity to see them play in person was overwhelming, and Henry laughed when I asked him if his dilapidated old car could go any faster.

When we arrived at the Wichita Sports Arena, there was excitement in the air as people milled around. We were all about to witness two of the best players in the world competing against one another. Henry had splurged on incredible seats, behind the baseline and about fifteen rows up. Although this was only an exhibition match, when Chris Conrad and Jake Sanders took the court to warm up, I was mesmerized.

As we watched the match, Henry quietly offered insight into several different areas. He had me watch a few points, focusing not on the ball, but on footwork only. We also examined the ball toss of each player to see how it varied from first serve to second serve. Henry clearly wanted me to understand that these remarkable athletes hadn't simply been "born with it."

We watched as Jake Sanders hit a blazing serve right up the middle, only to see it explode off Conrad's racket and land deep in the court. Moving effortlessly to his left, Sanders crunched a backhand crosscourt, which I was sure would be an outright winner. But lightening-quick Chris Conrad was able to reach the ball in time to tee off with his huge topspin forehand, absolutely ripping a forehand right up the line for a winner. The crowd exploded with applause, and I found myself jumping to my feet and cheering. Henry was a little more reserved and dignified, applauding politely, and grinning at me when I sat down.

"Good tennis, huh?"

My face registered astonishment and awe at what I was witnessing. I looked at Henry and whispered excitedly, "Remember when you talked about superstars programming their computers to be able to compete at the highest level possible? This is what you meant."

"Yep. We're watching live proof of what it takes to be great. When you look at their racket preparation, the bending, the follow-through, you know why these guys hit the ball so beautifully. It isn't magic, it's fundamentals and a lifetime of hard work."

Watching Chris Conrad and Jake Sanders perform with such grace and skill had been enlightening and inspirational. The next day I was back on the court, wondering if I could ever play like them. I had three weeks left until the start of school, and I would be spending the last two in Los Angeles, visiting my dad. I didn't want to lose the momentum my game had picked up during the summer, so I devoted myself to having my best week of practice ever with Henry. We spent that entire week drilling from dawn until dusk, and by Friday afternoon I was ready for my California vacation.

Los Angeles was a lot of fun—the beaches were amazing, the girls were pretty, and Lisa and Dad were happy to have us. Dad was really trying to make up for lost time because he took off two weeks of work while we were there. Brandon got to go to Disneyland and I did a lot of sightseeing, including a visit to the Los Angeles Tennis Club, where Henry used to work. It was truly a memorable trip.

Three days after I returned from California, I was walking down the corridor at Courage High on the first day of my sophomore year of high school. Jimmy Ellis snuck up behind me and punched me on the shoulder.

"Look, it's that movie star from L.A.! Can I have your autograph?" I laughed heartily, rubbing my shoulder.

"Jimmy, I wish you could have been there, man. That city is so cool. It's totally different from here."

"Dude, I've never even been outside of Kansas. Here you are, Mr. Hollywood. So, what do the ladies look like?"

"My dad's club has this huge swimming pool and the girls are in full effect."

Jimmy smiled, "Bryan, when you're a 'player' like me, the girls are always in full effect."

"Yeah right," I said. "I just hope 'player' is something you can put on a college application. Dude, what's the story with that, have you even started to think about what college you're going to honor with your presence?"

"Well, it's kind of hard to decide, with so many prestigious institutions knocking down my door." It was impossible to miss the sarcasm in Jimmy's voice. "My dad has been talking about me having a great year in tennis so I can get a scholarship, but I've never even played sectionals. Who's gonna want a player who's only ranked in Kansas?"

It was true that a ranking in a weak tennis state didn't carry too much weight. I knew that although Jimmy was a solid tennis player, he was probably small-college material at best. He had been blessed with natural athletic ability, but working on his game had never been a high priority for him. "So what are you gonna do, Jimmy?"

"I dunno, B." His tone cheered as he said, "No matter what happens, though, I'll still tax *your* butt on the tennis court."

I laughed, as the first period bell started to ring. A few minutes later, sitting in class, I shook my head as I thought, *Boy, did the summer go quickly!* It had started with the disappointment of the injury, but ended up being an action-packed three months, capped off with a great trip to Los Angeles. I thought it was cool of Dad to carve out some time for just him and me so that we could hang out and do stuff, like go to the beach and take a hike in the mountains overlooking the city. It gave us a chance to talk, and I was pretty straightforward about how I felt. I told him that I noticed—and appreciated—the genuine effort he was making. But I also told him about my friends' dads, men who were always there for their kids. I told him that I wanted him to be like that. He said that he was going to prove to me day by day that he was someone I could count on, regardless of what city he was living in. He even promised me that he'd make it to one of my tournament matches. I believed him, but I wasn't holding my breath.

Although Los Angeles was fantastic, I was glad to get back home, especially because Henry and I jumped right back into our training without missing a beat. One day we were doing a drill in which Henry would feed a ball from his huge basket to a corner, forcing me to run my hardest and hit the ball crosscourt. Then he would quickly feed another ball to the opposite corner, testing my ability to recover and hit on the run. It was extremely tiring, and at one point I was pulled so far wide that I didn't even go for the next ball, opting for a quick rest instead.

Henry stopped for a moment and said, "Bryan, I know you're beat. But still, never give up and concede a point like that. I want you to condition yourself to make the extra effort every single time."

I sighed, "But what do you do when your body finally says 'no more?'"

"Tell it to shut up." Henry smiled. "Obviously, everyone gets to that point eventually. But no matter how exhausted you are, you've got to believe that you can still reach down and find the energy to stay out there for a few more games. Bryan, one day you'll win a match that you have absolutely no business winning, just because you have the mental toughness to hang around and refuse to take 'no' for an answer. It'll be a wonderful feeling when you do."

"I'm with you, Henry," I said, taking a deep breath and getting in the ready position again.

"Okay, let's switch gears and pick up where we left off yesterday with your second serve."

I threw my arms up in mock despair, "No, not the second serve again!"

Henry laughed. We *had* been spending a great deal of time on it recently, but he felt it was one of the most important shots in tennis, often overlooked by most coaches.

"Bryan, have I ever told you the story of the conversation I had with the legendary Sam 'Grand Slam' Diamond?"

He had, many times. "I don't think so," I said, taking Elizabeth's advice and pretending it was a brand new story.

"He was one of the top servers in the 1940s. Even if he were down love-40, he would still be favored to win the game, against anybody in the world. Once, when I asked him what made his fabulous serve so effective, he totally surprised me by talking about—"

"His second serve!" I interrupted with a laugh, finishing Henry's story. "He could go for broke on his first serve, even on crucial points. If he missed, he still had the best second serve in the world to fall back on."

Henry chuckled. "I guess I have told that story a couple of times before. I remember it like it was yesterday. 'Grand Slam' looked right at me and said, 'Henry, as far as I'm concerned, *you're only as good as your second serve.*' I've never forgotten that statement."

At the end of September, I participated in the Oklahoma State Fall Junior Open, marking the first time I had ever traveled out of Kansas to play tennis. It gave me a sense of great satisfaction that I had finally moved into the challenging world of sectional play. Sectional tournaments were much tougher than state events because they included players from neighboring states, so the level of competition was naturally much higher. I lost in the first round, 7-5, 6-4, to a kid from Oklahoma named Joey McClain. The tennis was good, but McClain broke once in each set to win the match.

My second sectional tournament was the Mid-Town Junior Fall Classic, in Sioux City, Iowa. Once again, I played well but lost in the first round. Dave Coleman, the number six player in Nebraska, defeated me 6-4 in the third. Despite the fact that I had lost early in both tournaments, Henry was quite pleased.

"These experiences are gonna have a very positive impact on your game, kid."

"Yeah, but neither McClain nor Coleman even qualified for the nationals last year. There are much better guys than them."

"I know, but you'll get there. The top kids from your section may be a couple of levels above you right now, but you'll be surprised how quickly you can close the gap. The important thing is that you've made the transition into sectional play."

"I guess," I said, "but it was so frustrating because I had a chance to win both of those matches. If I'd just played a couple of points better, who knows what might have happened?"

"Bryan, there's a fine line between winning and losing in tennis. This reminds me of an expression I had that always helped Johnny in tight matches. I would tell him: 'The game that gets you there won't win it for you.' Do you understand what that means?"

I scratched my head, "Not really."

"It's actually pretty simple. Great players always seem to play their best when it counts the most, right?"

"Sure, that's what makes them so tough."

"Exactly. And because of that, you have to raise your game to the next level to close out a big match against that type of player."

I finished Henry's thought, knowing where he was going with this, "So great players have the ability to rise to the occasion. And if I don't raise my game in close matches, I'm gonna go down."

"That's why the superstars almost always get the close ones. In big-time tennis, you have to *win* the match, Bryan. Nobody is going to hand it to you. You have to go for it all."

One night in late November, two months after I had played my first sectional match, I sat at my desk reviewing my upcoming schedule. In addition to the usual state events, there were two important sectional tournaments on the horizon. One was the Junior Holiday Classic, held in Missouri in December. The other was the Winter Classic, held in Norman, Oklahoma, in early February. I hoped that one of these tournaments would provide me with my first win in sectional play.

There was one other date that was highlighted boldly on my calendar. January 15 marked the return of my favorite tournament, the Courage Open. The event had a special place in my heart because it always coincided with my birthday; this time around I was turning sixteen, a momentous birthday for any kid who wanted a driver's license.

But this year, even more significantly, the tournament would give me an opportunity to realize a dream—to show everybody in Courage, Kansas, that I had gotten better under the tutelage of my coach and friend, Henry Johnson.

CHAPTER NINE

THE PARTY

The blare of Jimmy's honking horn pierced the air loudly enough to be heard throughout the entire neighborhood. Grabbing my heavy jacket, I ran outside and jumped into his car on a snowy December night during winter break.

"What's up, dude?" Jimmy asked. He was dressed in jeans and a white T-shirt, with his hair slicked back. I was dressed similarly, although my dark brown hair was neatly combed and parted.

"Same ol', same ol', Jimmy. What's happening?"

"Robbie's parents are out of town. It's *on* tonight."

"I didn't hear anything at school about a big party."

Jimmy grinned, "We kept it quiet, otherwise everyone would have shown up."

We arrived at Robbie Helton's house to find that

"everyone" had shown up anyway. The party was in full swing. Some people were dancing to loud music while others stood around talking. The sounds of carefree laughter filled the air. I was one of the few sophomores who were in attendance tonight. The crowd consisted mainly of juniors and seniors, kids I didn't know beyond names and faces. Jimmy, of course, knew everyone, and after exchanging hellos with several of his friends, he led me over to a huge glass bowl that was filled with punch and ice cubes. "This is the good stuff," he declared. He poured a generous amount into a paper cup and took a long sip. He filled another cup for me, and I cautiously had a taste. It was good, but as I had suspected, it was spiked.

"What's in this, Jimmy?" I asked nervously.

"Just some gin to give it a little kick. Don't worry, it won't kill you."

I saw people looking at me, so I casually took another sip as though it was no big deal. I already had a reputation as a squeaky clean athlete—the last thing I wanted was people saying that I was also a nerd. The pressure was getting to me. I was surprised at how quickly my cup was empty. Jimmy refilled it and we walked toward the center of the room, where most of the activity was taking place. With another week of winter break remaining and a house overflowing with friends, the vibe was awesome.

By the time I finished my second cup of punch, I started to feel very relaxed and loose. I noticed Dylan Garrett, a senior I knew from the tennis team, hanging out by the punch bowl, so I sauntered over to say hi. We bumped knuckles and he insisted that I drink a cup of punch with him to celebrate his admission to the University of Kansas. I should have known better than to be drinking. After all, it was alcohol that ruined my parents' marriage, and alcohol that had caused so many problems for my father. I felt guilty, but that feeling quickly disappeared and was replaced by a new one: dizziness. I tried to make my way back to Jimmy, but all of a sudden the room was spinning and I bumped right into Adam Parker, whose drink spilled all over his shirt.

"Sorry 'bout that," I mumbled. A few people laughed at me.

"What do you think you're doing?" The varsity football player pushed my chest forcefully.

I snapped back at him, "What's your problem? I said sorry." Had I been sober, I never would have made such a confrontational comment, especially to someone as large as Adam.

"Sorry ain't good enough, sophomore." Parker looked at the people in his group. "Maybe somebody should teach our little tennis star a lesson about respecting his elders."

"Are you talking to my friend?" Jimmy was there in an instant. He had made regular trips back to the punch bowl, a factor that was now contributing to his fearless stance.

"This has nothing to do with you, Ellis. Stay out of it." Adam didn't even look at Jimmy.

"If it has something to do with a friend of mine, then I guess it does involve me. Don't you think? Or are you too dumb to think?" Jimmy emphasized the last sentence by poking two fingers into Parker's chest.

Now he had Adam's attention. "Maybe you're the one who needs to be taught a lesson."

"So teach me," was Jimmy's swaggering response.

All of a sudden things happened in a flash. Parker shoved Jimmy hard, knocking him off balance. Recovering quickly, Jimmy countered with a wild left hook that caught Parker square on the jaw. The sheer force of the punch caused the bulky football player to lose his footing. Jimmy leaped at him and they both fell to the ground, wrestling furiously. I was in a daze, watching the whole episode as though it was a slow motion scene from a movie. Everyone had gathered around to watch the fight. With the alcohol swirling around in my body, I felt like I was going to be sick.

When the fight was finally broken up, it was hard to distinguish the winner from the loser. Jimmy's shirt was torn, and he was clutching his bleeding hand, wincing. Parker looked even worse.

"Jimmy, is your hand okay?" I inspected it, and I could see that it was red and swollen. "Do you want me to get you some ice or something?"

"Naw, dude, I'm cool. I'll worry about it later."

"Thanks for sticking up for me."

"Don't worry about it. He's nothing but a punk who talks too much." Jimmy was glowing in the aftermath of the brawl. He was obviously a little drunk, and he seemed very pleased with himself. "Okay, Bryan, let's not stand here like losers. Let's party!" So we made our way back into the crowd, Jimmy basking in the glory of his scuffle, and me trying to concentrate on not puking.

By the time I got home, an hour past my curfew, my stomach felt like it was in the spin cycle of a washing machine.

It certainly didn't do my weakened condition any good to see the light in the living room, which told me that my mom had waited up.

"Bryan, do you have any idea how late it is!" Mom immediately smelled the alcohol on me. "Have you been drinking?"

"Um, well, yeah. I'm sorry, Mom. It's just that—"

"Bryan!" she yelled, "I don't even want to hear it! Go to your room at once and we'll talk about this in the morning."

I was so tired and sick that I crawled up the stairs and into my bedroom. I dropped onto my bed like a piece of luggage and fell asleep with all my clothes on. I slept until past noon the next day, a rare occurrence for me. When I woke up, I had a splitting headache, and to make matters worse, I realized that I had flaked on Henry. We had been scheduled to practice at 10:00 that morning. I walked into the kitchen, where Mom was waiting for me.

"Well, Bryan, now that you're up, we can finally talk. First of all, you're grounded. For a long time. I'm going to make sure that this lesson gets stuck in your head like one of your tennis lessons. We've talked about this subject many times before, that's why I'm so surprised. You know very well that alcohol destroyed our family."

"I know, Mom. It was stupid. The whole night was stupid. As a matter of fact, it wasn't even fun." I shook my head, "I just want to put this behind me and move forward with my life."

"Well a good place to start would be an explanation to your coach. He called a couple of hours ago."

I glanced at the clock on the wall. "Oh no. What'd you tell him?"

"I told him you were out on special assignment for the FBI—what do you *think* I told him? I explained how you came home drunk last night." Mom's voice was hard and cold. I groaned. My headache got a little worse when I tried to think about what Henry's reaction would be. "Bryan, I understand that sometimes kids are with their friends and there is pressure to fit in, but still, you know better. Look, your dad lost his job, his marriage broke up, and he's still trying to mend his relationship with his children. So you tell me if alcohol is a positive thing."

I was about to answer her when the doorbell rang. Brandon, who had been in the living room playing a computer game, opened the door and I heard him exclaim, "Dude, what happened to your hand?"

When I heard Jimmy's voice responding with a sarcastic comment that made Brandon laugh, I rushed from the kitchen to the front door and gasped when I saw Jimmy's left hand— his tennis hand. It was securely lodged in a hard cast, which extended up to his wrist.

Jimmy's crooked grin told the whole story. "What's up, Bry?" Jimmy noticed my mom in the kitchen and greeted her, "Hey, Mrs. B."

I was shocked and upset by the cast on Jimmy's hand. "This is all my fault. If I hadn't—"

"Whoa, hold on, Bryan. This is not your fault. I was totally out of control last night. I was supposed to concentrate on my tennis this year and try for a scholarship." He pointed to his cast, "Now I can kiss that goodbye."

"It must have been some party," Mom called out from the kitchen. "How did this happen?"

"Well let's put it this way," Jimmy said grimacing, "I learned that I have a tremendous left hook and that Adam Parker's jaw is made out of steel."

Mom forced a smile and Jimmy and I walked into the living room to talk. He became serious when we sat down. "You know what? I've done way too much partying, and not nearly enough work on the court, or in my classes. I really admire you, Bry."

"What do you mean?" I asked.

"You know, the way you've stuck with it and worked hard. I know I never admit to it, but you're a much better player than me now, and I'm proud of you." He tapped his cast lightly against his head for effect. "I've gotta get my act together. It's all good, though. I know I've been kind of a screw-up, but this whole thing has opened my eyes." There was an uncomfortable pause, but then "serious" Jimmy became "sarcastic and funny" Jimmy again, "I guess I should thank you for being partly responsible for me breaking my hand."

"Glad I was able to be so helpful."

"Now that I've got this stupid cast to deal with and I can't play in the Courage Open, who knows, Bryan, you might actually have a shot."

"Yeah, if Henry doesn't kill me first for missing practice."

Jimmy checked his watch, "Speaking about getting killed, I gotta go. I'm grounded for the next thirty years, so I'll

83

see you when I'm like fifty."

I laughed as Jimmy closed the door behind him with his good hand. And in spite of the fact that my mom ultimately decided upon a severe punishment for me, too, she spared me from the one thing I had feared the most: restricting my tennis. I could forget about getting my driver's license for a long time, or going out on weekends for the foreseeable future. But there was no restriction on my participation in the Courage Open, which was less than three weeks away. I was grateful to Mom, because in my mind this was no ordinary Courage Open. This was my time to show and prove.

CHAPTER TEN

THE RETURN OF THE COURAGE OPEN

My considerable improvement had been noted by The Courts tournament committee, which had seeded me fourth in the Courage Open. I was very proud about it, but I was acutely aware of the pressure that accompanied high expectations. At 9:00 on the morning of January 15, I walked up the stairs to the spacious lounge, smiling when I saw Judy Fletcher at the desk. Good old reliable Mrs. Fletcher! I got in line behind a couple of people who were checking in. When they left, Judy gave me a big smile.

"Well, here we are again, Bryan."

"Yep. And this time I'm gonna go further than I did last year—I hope."

"I hope so too, Bryan."

I gathered my things and sat down on one of the couches by the window. Henry, who was usually punctual, arrived a few minutes late. "Sleep in this morning?" I kidded.

Henry smiled, "Yes, as a matter of fact, but I'm more worried about *you* falling asleep during your first round."

I laughed, "Yeah, they gave me Larry Cooper."

"Bryan, even though he doesn't pose a challenge, it's still important to play hard and keep your concentration. If you play some loose points out of sympathy, one day you'll play a loose point when it actually matters."

I followed Henry's instructions and dispatched Cooper love and love in forty minutes. When I got upstairs, I found Henry and two men involved in a heated discussion about the movie business. Henry was loudly proclaiming that the movies of the 1930s and 1940s were far more sophisticated and intriguing than the uninspired action flicks of current times. Chuckling to myself, I walked over to the large window to check out Mike Scully's first-round match on court number one.

About ten minutes later, Henry joined me at the window. We watched as Scully methodically dismantled his opponent. Henry shook his head after Scully hit a drop volley winner with the finesse of a champion. "A great player, and an even nicer man. I wish you could have seen him in the juniors, Bryan, he was terrific."

"Yeah, that's what I've heard."

"It's all true. Anyway, let's talk about your match with Foster, so you can get something to eat and relax before you play again."

A few hours later, I was warming up with Bill Foster, feeling loose and confident. After we took our practice serves, I held up a ball, indicating that I was ready to begin. As the match progressed, a high percentage of my first serves were finding their target, enabling me to hold with ease. When Foster served, I moved in and caught the return early, hitting the ball at his feet time and time again. He was regarded as a good player because of an effective serve and volley, but he was obviously unaccustomed to such precise returns of serve. He finally stopped rushing the net altogether, an ill-advised decision, because off the ground he wasn't nearly as proficient as me. A match that would have once frightened me was now routine, 6-2, 6-1.

"Bryan, you were marvelous today!" My mom embarrassed me with a big hug as I came up the stairs. Henry offered his customary, "Good work, kid."

My mom turned to Henry and said, "You've done quite a job, Mr. Johnson. Bryan looked super out there."

"Yeah, but he was playing another bum. Let's see how he looks tomorrow, when things get tougher."

I smiled. That was classic Henry—making sure I didn't get a swelled head. "Nine-thirty tomorrow morning, Henry."

"Good, kid, I'll see you here. Don't forget to stretch. Have a nice afternoon, Mrs. Berry."

With the day of tennis comfortably behind me, I went with Mom to watch Brandon's basketball game. Although I was a little nervous, I had a good feeling about the way I was playing. I desperately wanted to defeat my next opponent, Keith Nichols, because that would put me in the quarters for the first time ever. As an added bonus, a very familiar foe would probably await me. The withdrawal of Jimmy Ellis had opened up the draw for Ted Grover, who was sailing his way through the early rounds.

I was excited by the fact that Grover and I were on a collision course to meet up again. It would be a fiercely competitive match, but I felt that I was up to the challenge. I had waited a long time for a rematch—I figured I owed him one.

The next morning I was back in action out on court number four. Keith Nichols, a shrewd counterpuncher, seemed content to keep the ball in the court, hoping perhaps that I would grow impatient and go for too much. But Nichols had seriously underestimated the kind of pressure that Henry had taught me to apply. Although some of the points were long and well played, I frequently hit winners or sizzling approaches that set up easy opportunities. To even my own surprise, I marched into the quarterfinals in a rout, 6-3, 6-1.

"Good work, kid, you looked sharp out there. How do you feel?"

"I feel great, Henry. Ready for Ted Grover."

Henry laughed, "I'm glad to hear that, because he won his match. It's you and him at two o'clock. Everybody's already talking about it."

"Cool." I was pleased, although I felt a quick wave of nervousness run right through me.

When I found myself warming up on court number one with Ted Grover, I couldn't have felt more excited. After all, this was the first time that I had ever been scheduled on the main court. With a victory today, my arrival at The Courts would be solidified. As for Grover, a win over me would be the defining moment of his tennis career, especially because a large crowd was watching from the lounge upstairs.

As we concluded our warm-ups, Grover seemed strangely reserved—he knew that he wasn't playing the same kid that he had humbled twice in the last twelve months. In addition to a new serve, my erratic, flat forehand had been replaced by a blistering topspin forehand. Also, as a result of Henry's relentless training methods, I felt as though I could literally fly around the court. Not to mention the fact that I now stood a full six-feet-tall, and was a stronger and more confident version of Bryan Berry. Of course, the biggest difference between this year and last year was also the most meaningful. I was fortunate enough to have a trusted mentor who I could rely on for guidance and support. The old man was always there for me as a coach, but more significantly, as a friend.

As the quarterfinals of the Courage Open got under way, the spectators settled in to watch a tightly contested grudge match between opponents who clearly didn't like one another. But it never materialized. When Grover came to net, passing shots whizzed by him as though they had been shot from a cannon. When he rallied from the baseline, precision groundstrokes left him totally flat-footed. When he tried to hit passing shots, I blanketed the net and hit crisp volley winners. Grover's bad line calls and disruptive antics served no purpose other than to make him look like a fool.

Last year, Grover had caused me to experience one of my most disheartening moments ever in tennis. It had taken a long time and countless hours of hard work, but I finally claimed my revenge. Playing with a heightened sense of passion and determination, I started beating up on Ted Grover from the very first point, delivering a ruthless 6-1, 6-0 knockout.

The final point of the match was especially sweet. I was toying with Grover, hitting the ball easy to extend the rally. I was waiting for something I could clobber, like the tennis equivalent of a batting-practice fastball right down the middle. And Grover unwittingly offered it up. After we had exchanged about ten balls, he tried to hit a winner up my forehand line. But I anticipated it easily and got there in a flash. Loading up the topspin forehand that Henry had taught me, I assaulted the tennis ball, hitting it so hard up the line that a beaten-down Grover didn't even try for it. He just stood and stared for a second. Now that my mission was finally complete, I raised my fist and let out a loud, triumphant yell. I had nothing to say to Grover—my tennis had done all the talking. But I did shoot a defiant glance directly at Harry Benson and Neil Avery, who were watching me from the lounge. My stare was payback for the cruel comments they had made about Henry nine months earlier.

Before leaving with my family, I spent a few minutes alone with Henry, who was generous with his praise. Although the old man was a stickler about court etiquette, he didn't even admonish me for my uncharacteristic outburst at the end of the match. He understood. We were both excited because I was now in the semifinals of the Courage Open. *The semis.* That had a nice ring to it.

As we were saying good-bye, I casually reached into my tennis bag and handed Henry the gift that I had hidden in there. It was a card that I had made on my computer a couple of nights earlier. I had hoped that I could give it to Henry under these exact circumstances.

The front of the card was a drawing of two people, an older man and a teenager, standing in front of a crudely sketched building with a sign that said "The Courts." They were both smiling and holding tennis rackets. I had patterned the card after the picture of Henry and Johnny in front of the Los Angeles Tennis Club. When Henry opened up the card to look on the inside, he found the following words:

Dear Henry,

I never get around to saying thank you for all the wonderful things you do for me. Your support and encouragement give me the strength to get out there and work hard every day. I know I've got a long way to go, but you've taught me to believe in what we're doing. It's difficult to imagine what type of tennis player I would have become if I hadn't been fortunate enough to benefit from your knowledge and insight. More importantly, it's almost impossible to imagine what type of person I would be without your friendship. So I want to express my sincere appreciation by offering a heartfelt thank you. I also want to explain why I'm giving you this card today, since it's not your birthday or anything. It was one year ago today that you came over and talked to me for the very first time, and started teaching me. It's a day I'll always remember.

Your friend forever,

Bryan

Six days later the four semifinalists assembled at The Courts, ready to do battle. There had been no surprises thus far; the tournament had gone true to form, as everyone had been eliminated other than the top four seeds. But I was faced with the biggest challenge of all—I had to test my skills against the perennial favorite, the greatest player in the history of Courage, Mike Scully!

The first match of the day was scheduled for noon, featuring me against Scully. It would be followed immediately by Alex Warner vs. Kenny Singleton to round out the semifinals. The two winners would meet the next day for the championship.

This was by far the most exposure I had ever received at The Courts. More than fifty spectators were lined up around court number one, in addition to the overflowing crowd in the lounge upstairs. Obviously there was genuine interest in watching an up-and-coming junior take on the reigning champion.

I had spent the last couple of hours with Henry, relaxing and talking quietly. The old man was very low-key, trying to prevent me from getting too nervous. After going over the game plan, he handed me a piece of paper that was folded over a couple of times. "What's this?"

"It's nothing, Bryan, don't even think about it. Just stick it in your pocket and take a quick peek at it after the first set. Now, let's go over strategy again."

When it was time for our match, Scully greeted me warmly at the desk. As we made our way down to court one, he could tell how nervous and intimidated I was. He made some small talk in an effort to help me feel a little more relaxed, "Nice job getting to the semis. I saw the end of your match with Grover. You sure let him have it."

"Yeah, Grover's never really been too friendly to me, so that win felt pretty good."

Scully smiled, "I know what you're saying. I used to play singles with him when I was about twelve or thirteen. They didn't even have The Courts back then. We used to play over in Mill Valley. He was just as obnoxious then as he is now!"

As we were warming up, I tried to forget about the situation and concentrate on hitting the ball smoothly. But my mind lapsed as I silently acknowledged the beauty of Scully's game. He was a *player*, as Henry liked to say. After we had taken our serves, Scully held up a ball and I nodded. As the match began, I was so nervous that I missed four straight returns. We switched sides and Scully quickly broke serve to make it 2-love.

By the time I was serving at love-5, I was simply trying to make a respectable showing. Winning wasn't even the issue anymore. I had looked up at Henry, who was watching from his customary spot in the lounge upstairs. As usual, there was no expression on the old man's face. I felt powerless as Scully continued to hit superb shots effortlessly. Just like that, the first set was over. It had taken barely twenty minutes for the bagel to be served up.

After Scully held easily to open the second set, I started to walk to the other side of the court to change ends. As I did, I glanced up at Henry, who was frantically motioning to his pocket and then pointing at me. The piece of paper! I had forgotten all about it. Slipping it out of my pocket, I quickly toweled off and took a swig from a bottle of water. I unfolded the paper and looked at it. One sentence was printed in Henry's handwriting: *"If you're afraid to lose, you can't win."*

As I slowly picked up a ball and prepared to serve, I gazed at Henry. Even from a distance, I could feel the intensity as the old man nodded slightly. The message was clear: win or lose, it was time to stop playing scared. But in spite of my predicament, I did have to smile for a second. How could Henry have possibly known that I was going to be in need of something to get me back on track?

Tossing the ball high up in the air, I finally hit my serve, blasting it down the center. The pace caught Scully off guard, but he was still able to flick a one-handed backhand deep in the court. I slid over to my left and looped my two-handed backhand crosscourt. Scully was there, slicing a backhand and rushing to the net, but I anticipated it perfectly. I lifted an offensive topspin lob that was just out of his extended reach, landing softly right on the baseline. The crowd cheered and I pumped my fist. *Now we're talkin'!*

All of a sudden, now that Henry had given me a necessary jolt, the complexion of the match changed dramatically.

My furious onslaught was a real challenge for my opponent, who had been breezing comfortably. The intensity picked up, and Scully could not ignore the fact that this had turned into a tennis match. The torrid pace continued without pause until we were deadlocked at 6-all. I had forced Mike Scully into a tiebreaker! The second set was now nearly an hour old.

The crowd had really gotten involved in the match, hooting and hollering loudly with every great shot. They were clearly enjoying this exhibition of competition and skill. Scully was always looking for an opportunity to get to the net, but he was forced to be selective now that I was hitting with depth and accuracy. When we both stayed back, the points were long and exciting.

During the tiebreaker, the level of tennis didn't fade. Mike Scully, who had played professionally, was well acquainted with the concept of handling pressure. I, on the other hand, was still learning. At 3-all, Scully raised his game a couple of notches, suddenly hitting the ball with even more authority and urgency. I didn't ease up, but a former world-class player was drawing on all of his experience and skill. Scully played the last four points like a true champion, overwhelming me with a flurry of powerful combinations. He captured the tiebreaker 7-3, and the match 6-0, 7-6.

Henry later said that Scully had demonstrated the meaning of the expression, "The game that gets you there won't win it for you." Still, Henry was pleased, saying that the best way to learn these types of lessons was through real-life tournament experience.

When I shook hands with Mike at the net, I was smiling broadly. I knew I had accomplished something important today, so this was one defeat I wasn't going to take hard. It was gratifying to realize how much progress I had made in such a short time. Henry's training methods were very demanding, but I wasn't the complaining kind. Henry had paid me the ultimate compliment by saying that my dedication to the sport equaled only one other kid—his magnificent original protégé, Johnny Matthews. He also told me that the card I had given him was something he would treasure until the day he died.

A word of praise from Mike Scully was like icing on the cake, "Bryan, that was incredible! When I saw you play Grover, I knew you were hitting the ball well and that you had improved tremendously. But to tell you the truth, until today, I didn't realize how good you'd gotten."

Until this day, neither had I.

CHAPTER ELEVEN

PREPARING FOR BATTLE

One night in late May, I sat at my computer listening to some music after finishing my homework. I was reflecting upon the dizzying pace of the last few months. Henry and I had been working harder than ever, shooting for the goal that had eluded us the previous summer—a chance to go to the nationals.

As the number two sixteen-year-old in Kansas, a ranking that had come as a result of my stellar play over the previous year, I believed that I was a legitimate contender. I had once told Henry that my dream was to have the opportunity to compete against the best players in the entire country. But to earn that right, I would first have to encounter the premier players from five states in a pressure-packed, three-week series of tournaments known as the Missouri Valley Supers Circuit. Based on the results of these three tournaments, a selection committee would choose six kids and endorse them to move on to the nationals. The USTA, United States Tennis Association, had divided the country into seventeen different sections, each one consisting of one or more states, depending on size and geographical location. My section, the Missouri Valley Section, included players from Iowa, Nebraska, Kansas, Oklahoma, and Missouri. The six players that emerged from the Missouri Valley Section would have the privilege of joining fewer than two hundred other kids from across the United States who had triumphed in similar qualifying tournaments. These juniors—America's finest—would come together to do battle at the time-honored Super National Championship tournaments.

The prospect of competing with the most accomplished kids from my section was both exciting and scary. With everyone vying for one of the six sectional endorsements to go to the nationals, the stakes at the Missouri Valley Supers circuit simply couldn't be higher. Adding to the pressure was the knowledge that after the first two tournaments, only sixteen players would be selected to participate in the final tournament. The selection committee used this rooting-out process to set the stage for the single most important sectional event of the year, the Missouri Valley Sweet Sixteen tournament. I knew that I would have to reach new heights to have a chance. But I was heartened by the fact that I had finally broken through in sectional play, reaching the round of sixteen in each of my last two tournaments.

So overall I felt great about everything. I was hitting the ball better than ever, my confidence level was high, and most importantly, I was injury free. I had several good players to practice with, including Jimmy, whose rehabilitation was finally complete after the serious injury to his hand. His tennis wasn't nearly as sharp as it had once been, but he seemed to be a happier and more focused kid. With steadily improving grades, getting into a decent college appeared to be a realistic goal. And, in the spirit of making positive changes, he had also stopped drinking.

I certainly didn't need any further evidence about the negative effects of alcohol. The party had left me so sick to my stomach that my tennis had suffered for a couple of days. I had come clean with Henry, whose reaction had been surprisingly mild. Instead of a lecture, the old man was able to get his point across very clearly with one of his inimitable remarks. He simply said, "Stay away from the sauce, kid. It'll cool the fire in your belly."

The only thing dampening my enthusiasm was that Henry had come down with a bad case of the flu and was bedridden at home. When I visited him, though, Henry didn't want to talk about his weakened condition. As always, he insisted on putting my tennis first. With the Missouri Valley Supers Circuit only a week away, the old man instructed me to call Mike Scully and ask him for some help.

I had been a little reluctant. "Henry, we've been together for a year-and-a-half. I don't know if I can be out there working with Mike, or anybody else."

"Bryan," Henry stated emphatically, "after all the work we've done together, and all the goals we've shot for, this is the time for you to play your best tennis. I wish I didn't have this stupid flu right now, but whether I'm in the stands watching, or lying around in my pajamas at home, I'm still with you. And I always will be."

"Okay, Henry, whatever you say. But Mike's a busy guy, I don't know if he'll even want to help me train for these tournaments."

"I think you're gonna be surprised, kid."

As usual, Henry's uncanny intuition was right on the money. Upon hearing about the situation, Mike Scully immediately agreed to help me out. He said that he'd been very unhappy working in the real estate business the last few years, prompting him to consider a return to tennis. Working with me was the perfect opportunity for him to see whether or not he would enjoy coaching. So with Mike on board, I was able to continue my training without disruption in preparation for the upcoming tournaments.

When I walked into the lounge area of the Oklahoma City Tennis Center the following Saturday, I could feel the electricity in the air. I gazed at the impressive gathering of talent as if I were a fan rather than a competitor. The best kids from five states! All of them were ready to begin the three most significant weeks of the year—the Missouri Valley Supers Circuit. The lounge was crowded and bustling with activity. The atmosphere was tense.

"Drew Phillips, Bryan Berry, report to the tournament desk please." It was time. I collected the balls, and then accompanied the seventh seed out to court four. Drew Phillips was huge—190 pounds of sheer muscle on a six-foot-two-inch frame. His game, while extremely erratic, was dangerous because he was a big hitter who wasn't afraid to aim for the lines.

I had been a bundle of nerves all day in anticipation of this match. But now that I was finally out on the court, I actually felt pretty relaxed. When Phillips held up a ball, indicating that he was ready to serve, I nodded, blocking everything else out of my mind. He tossed the ball into the air and swung—the tournament was under way! I was able to catch the ball early and return his serve with a low, skidding shot that forced him out of position. All Phillips could do was reach out and punch the ball toward the middle of the court, where it landed softly and at shoulder height. I ran around my backhand and loaded up my looping topspin forehand, ripping it crosscourt for a clean winner. *Thanks Henry!* Because of him, I was no longer the same kid who once had a shaky forehand that broke down under pressure.

The tennis was high quality, with neither of us backing down. But I seemed to have an answer on all the decisive points, and when the dust settled, I had racked up a convincing 7-5, 6-4 victory. I couldn't remember ever hitting the ball so crisply, so proficiently. A smile of satisfaction creased my face as I walked back to report the scores. I did belong here with all these excellent tennis players! All my doubts seemed to vanish with this one sparkling performance. I now knew that I could compete with anybody in my section, and I couldn't wait to get back out on the court and prove it.

I fought my way to the quarters before finally falling to the number two seed, Billy Richardson. We had a great match, a tough three-setter that seesawed back and forth until the very end. I was starting to climb to a new level, and it took some inspired tennis from Richardson to subdue me, 6-3 in the third.

I returned to Courage determined to keep the momentum going. One more solid showing would certainly place me among the sixteen who would be invited to play the all-important Missouri Valley Sweet Sixteen tournament. I eagerly looked forward to the next event, working hard with Mike Scully to prepare for it.

Six days later I was in Waterloo, Iowa, for the second leg of the circuit. After a surprisingly easy first-round victory, I squared up against Craig Schroeder of Missouri, a fierce baseliner who weighed in as the fifth seed. A short, skinny kid, Schroeder neither served hard nor ventured to net. He didn't make very many mistakes either. His reputation as a tenacious competitor had been validated the previous week when he battled his way to the semis.

The points in this round of sixteen match were long and well played. Schroeder was a resourceful counterpuncher, and winning a baseline rally from him required concentration and patience. All those long sessions with the old man were paying off because I felt strong and alert even after two hours had elapsed. This was a severe challenge, including the ultimate danger of facing a match point! After dropping the first set, I was serving at 4-5, 30-40, in the second set. Beads of sweat dripped down my forehead and splashed onto the court. This was what I had trained for, playing a perfect point when I needed it most. I went for a big first serve that caught the tape and veered off to the sideline. Breathing deeply, I tossed the ball high into the air for what I knew would be the most crucial second serve of my entire life. If I double faulted here, the match was over! Thank goodness Henry had worked so hard with me on my second serve.

I hit it perfectly, just like I used to with Henry shouting over my shoulder. It traveled through the air with enough spin to easily clear the net, but it landed too deep for Schroeder to do much with it. He simply stroked the ball back with topspin, setting off yet another long baseline rally. I didn't go for too much, because this was obviously not the time to make a silly error. Instead, I stayed in the point with solid, deep shots, waiting and hoping for a good opportunity. My patience was finally rewarded when Schroeder hit a backhand that landed much shorter than he intended. With no hesitation whatsoever, I pounded the ball crosscourt and charged the net like a rampaging bull. Out of position and faced with a difficult shot, Schroeder tried to pass me up the line, but I was right there for the easy winner. Whew! I had survived a match point against me. Relieved and inspired, I went on a tear. When it was finally over, I had come away with the biggest sectional win of my life, 3-6, 7-5, 6-4. I had taken out the fifth seed!

Later that evening I sat in my room at the Waterloo Inn, reflecting upon my situation. With my win today, I'd already beaten a couple of high caliber players on the way to the quarters in two straight events. I felt that I was all but certain to get an invitation to the Missouri Valley Sweet Sixteen tournament. If so, fifteen other players and I would engage in one final battle to determine the recipients of the six golden tickets—the coveted sectional endorsements to play the nationals!

Perhaps I was a little too relaxed the next day, because I just couldn't get anything going. Eric Davis, the number four seed, was merciless in an attack that led to a 6-1, 6-2 rout. I felt uncharacteristically sluggish during this lackluster performance, which left me saddled with some nervous doubts. Would this loss erase the good things I had already done?

When we spoke on the phone that evening, Henry didn't want to dwell on this one bad day. I had completed a highly successful two weeks, proving that I could play with anyone in the section. My fate was now in the hands of the selection committee.

Henry clearly wasn't too worried. I had beaten some solid players, most of who would probably end up at the Missouri Valley Sweet Sixteen tournament. He felt sure that I would be chosen among the top sixteen.

I got the news the next morning, as Mom, Brandon, and I were packing up our things and getting ready to check out of the hotel. When the phone rang, I leaped at it and took it into the bathroom so I could have a little privacy. I spoke briefly with Mr. Jenkins from the selection committee and then hung up the phone and walked back into the room. I lowered my eyes and cast a despondent glance at Brandon and my mom, who were taken aback. After a moment, I cracked a big smile as I playfully grabbed Brandon. "Just kidding, bro, we're in!" An hour later we were back on the road to Courage. My dream was still alive.

CHAPTER TWELVE

THE FINAL PIECE OF
THE PUZZLE

After dropping off my stuff at home, I wasted no time getting over to Henry's house. When I walked through the front door, he was sitting on a chair in the living room covered in a thick blanket.

"Hey Henry, how ya feeling?"

"Like an old man. How are you, kid?" He smiled broadly, "Ready to play the Sweet Sixteen?"

"I don't know…it just doesn't seem real. I keep waiting for someone to wake me up and tell me that it's all a dream."

"Oh this is no dream," the old man spoke through a heavy cough. "Didn't I tell you all the hard work would pay off?"

I laughed, "I don't remember, Henry. You were too busy

yelling at me!" After about thirty minutes of giving Henry details about the tournaments and answering his questions, I left his house. I could have talked his ear off all night but I knew he needed to rest.

During the following five days, I worked out with Mike Scully in final preparation for the tournament. Mike was a welcome source of encouragement and insight. Henry had shown good instinct by pairing us together. The old man was pleased to see Mike take such an active role, feeling that I could learn a great deal from the former pro player. Obviously Henry was irreplaceable, but unfortunately he was still laid up and, truth be told, he didn't look like he was getting much better. I figured that it just took older people a lot longer to recover.

When I found myself on center court at the Wichita Tennis Club, I was downright nervous. I had been dreaming about the nationals for years; now I was one of sixteen kids who held it firmly within their grasp. This tournament was the final piece of the puzzle.

My opponent in this round of sixteen match was the number six seed, Peter Campbell, a lefty with a powerful game. Campbell, the number two player in Nebraska, seemed to have only one real deficiency, his slice backhand. I picked up on it early, after Campbell had blasted a couple of forehand winners to take the opening game. After he then hit a winner off my hardest first serve, I realized that I had to change up my game plan or I'd be hitting the showers early. *Man, does this guy have a huge forehand!* Taking a moment to adjust the strings on my racket, I thought about what Henry had taught me about this type of player. *A big hitter loves pace. Make him create his own pace!*

So that's what I did. At love-15, I kicked a serve shoulder high to his backhand, causing him to slice the ball meekly over the net. Instead of trying to blast a winner, I hit it deep to his backhand again. He returned it, but he was clearly out of his comfort zone. When I went back to it for the third time, his slice attempt was too low, catching the tape and swerving out of play. Gaining confidence, I ruthlessly continued to employ this strategy. Campbell's normally aggressive game faltered. Other than the times when he could run around his backhand and hit a forehand, I was completely in control. My persistent attack wore the lefty down, causing him to offer up weak, floating backhands time and time again. The match went my way, 7-5, 7-5.

Mike Scully, who was in attendance, was extremely pleased. "That was a major-league exhibition of skill, Bryan. You found his weakness and you exploited it. Now you've got some real momentum, so stay focused and don't let up."

The next day I drew Ricky Segal, the third seed. The top gun from Iowa for the second straight year, Segal was a calm and collected tennis player who was playing some big-time ball. He had earned one of our section's endorsements the previous year, so he already had experience at the national level. A win over him would be monumental.

The match was an instant classic between two sixteen-year-olds with bright futures ahead of them. But for me, there was something even more significant about this match: my dad was there. He had called me up a week earlier to tell me that he was taking a few days off of work and was going to fly out to see me play. I was more excited than ever to get out on the court.

With Dad and Mom sitting in the stands, and Brandon wedged strategically in between them, the match began. Segal won the first set 7-6, 10-8 in the tiebreaker. But I fought back, refusing to die. I won the second set 6-4, and we played to the wire in the third. Before the start of the deciding tiebreaker, I exchanged glances with Mike Scully in the stands. I remembered our tiebreaker at the Courage Open, when Mike's incredible performance reinforced the lesson that Henry had once taught me. *The game that gets you there won't win it for you.*

Henry would have been proud if he had seen the exciting conclusion of this epic two-and-a-half hour struggle. Segal was playing well, but I willed myself to raise the level of my game, taking some calculated risks. The biggest one was on the opening point of the tiebreaker, when I took a second serve from Segal and charged forward, attacking the net. He must have been shocked, because I hadn't done that once in the entire match. Unsure of himself, he hit a high topspin lob, but it wasn't very deep at all. I let it bounce and easily pounded an overhead winner. With the opening point of the tiebreaker in the bag, I confidently hit a couple of heavy first serves, jumping out to a quick 3-0 lead. I continued to stay aggressive, riding the momentum to the most important victory of my career, 7-3 in the tiebreaker, 7-6 in the third set.

When I walked off the court and my dad gave me a big hug, it made me feel really good. This was the first time he had seen me play a tournament match in a long time and I think he was shocked by how much I'd improved.

"You were amazing. I've never seen anything like it." Dad was smiling from ear to ear. For the first time in my life I could tell that he was truly proud of me. Still, it frustrated me that he was so surprised by my tennis skills. If he had been a part of my life for the past five years, he would have seen me steadily progressing, the way that Mom had. She was happy I played well, but there was no surprised expression on her face. Dad looked over at her and they shared the first smile between them in a long time.

"Kathleen, he really played like a pro out there, didn't he?" Mom nodded knowingly.

Even though Dad was busy with Lisa and his job, he had made several trips back to Kansas since his move to Los Angeles almost a year earlier. After that day in court, he'd told me that he was going to be a permanent part of my life, and so far he had been true to his word. He had promised that he would make it to one of my matches, and now he had. His reappearance into my life was starting to slowly erase the painful memories of a childhood without a real father. But the hard truth was that I was still not fully able to embrace our relationship. It was almost like I kept expecting my dad to fall back to his old ways. For now, though, he was acting like a normal dad, in spite of the fact that I wasn't giving a whole lot back to him. He said he understood, and that he had the rest of his life to regain my trust. But I wondered if I would ever be able to trust him again.

As happy as I was to have Dad there to watch me play, it was never far from my mind that someone else had been missing for a while now. *Henry, if only you could have been here to see this awesome victory.*

But there was something I didn't know. While I had been battling out there on the court, Henry was also engaged in a battle...for his *life*. That very same day, my mentor, an old man who meant more to me than anything, had suffered a major heart attack. Everything was about to change.

When I got home that afternoon and found the message on the answering machine from Elizabeth Johnson, I rushed straight over to Maywood Memorial Hospital. Sprinting down the hall of the third floor, I found Elizabeth standing at the registration desk talking quietly to a nurse. She turned to me as I approached, embracing me tightly. "Thanks for coming, Bryan." Elizabeth's face was ashen and she looked very weak. "Henry didn't want you to know until after you played your match."

"What happened?" My voice was barely audible.

"It was about six o'clock this morning," Elizabeth said. "Henry tried to get up to go to the bathroom and suddenly I heard him fall to the floor. I called 911 and the paramedics rushed him straight to the hospital."

I asked fearfully, "Will he...will he be okay?"

Elizabeth looked at me for a long moment. "Bryan, they're not sure. He's stable right now, but he's very sick. Remember, Henry is eighty-four years old."

I knew it, although sometimes it was the easiest thing in the world to forget. When I had first met Henry, I had assumed that the old man was only in his mid-seventies. But it had turned out that Henry's energy and vitality totally belied his age.

"Can I see him?" The nurse cast a disapproving look,

but Elizabeth smiled softly, "Go ahead, Bryan. If I know that old man, talking to you about tennis will be better medicine than anything they have at this hospital."

She was right. Henry didn't even give me a chance to say anything. His face was tired and drawn, but his eyes lit up when he saw me. In a hoarse voice that was close to a whisper, he asked, "How'd you do?"

"Henry," I replied, "I won it for you today, seven-six in the third over the number three seed. We're in the semis." Although Henry could barely keep his eyes open, I could see the satisfaction in his face. And when I touched his hand just before I left, the old man smiled at me.

The next day, I was back at the Wichita Tennis Club facing the top seed, Cory Marshall. As the number one sixteen-year-old from the Missouri Valley Section, Marshall was known as an experienced, skilled player who performed with the precision of a surgeon. Along with a successful debut in the national sixteens the previous summer, his résumé included a top twenty-five national ranking from the fourteens. He was the best junior I had ever played, and a lock to get one of the six sectional endorsements.

The tennis was excellent. Everybody, including Cory Marshall, figured out quickly that I was a man on a mission. But Cory responded with an inspired effort of his own. Producing some masterful tennis, the top seed earned a hard-fought, impressive 7-5, 6-4 win.

Two nights later I was sitting in Henry's hospital room, feeling depressed. I would have gladly exchanged every win of my life for the joy of having Henry back out on the court. I looked around the room. It was small and a little drab, but Elizabeth had brightened it up with a cheerful arrangement of flowers and balloons. My contribution was an old tennis racket, which was adorned with tennis balls that I had painted with happy faces. A banner was spread across the racket that read "Get well soon, Henry."

"You're quiet tonight, kid. Everything all right?"

"Yeah, I guess I'm just a little tired."

"Well, you've got a right to be. You've played a lot of tennis these last couple of weeks and I'm proud of you." Even in the face of a perilous medical situation, Henry seemed to be in good spirits.

"Do you think it will it be enough to get us over the top?"

Henry smiled weakly. That question had been on our minds for the last two days. "Until we hear which six they're sending, all we can do is wait."

"That's harder than actually playing the tennis."

Henry chuckled, "You can say that again. But look, you did your job, you went deep into every tournament, and you scored a couple of big wins. I don't know what else you could have done."

"Yeah, but there are a bunch of other guys who did really well over the past three weeks also."

"I know, Bryan." Henry looked at me for a long moment. "You're on the bubble and it could go either way. Life is like that sometimes."

The next day lasted an eternity. I had been informed that I could call the sectional office at 9:00 the following morning to find out the results of the selection process. On Henry's advice, I took the day off from tennis to give my tired body a little rest. I was able to distract myself by hanging out with my friends, but by bedtime I was just too hyped to fall asleep. In a few hours I would know if I was going to the nationals, something I had dreamed about for many years. Yet, while it was so close, it wasn't my principal concern. I tried not to think about it, but I knew deep down that Henry was very old and very sick. What was going to happen?

I made the call to the sectional office the instant I woke up. By 9:30, I arrived at the hospital, where Henry and Elizabeth were talking softly. She had already been there for several hours. We chatted for a few minutes, and then Elizabeth got up to get a cup of coffee from the hospital cafeteria.

Henry didn't say a word. He just looked at me and waited. He was an old man who knew he didn't have much time left, but his eyes burned with the intensity that I had grown so accustomed to. He had worked every bit as hard as I had over the past eighteen months. I sometimes joked that Henry had even outworked me.

I had printed out the six selections of the committee, titling the page "Missouri Valley Section Endorsements for Boys Sixteens." Without a word I held the list in front of Henry's face:

1. Cory Marshall
2. Billy Richardson
3. Ricky Segal
4. Eric Davis

5. Craig Schroeder

6. Bryan Berry

Henry was silent for a moment, overcome with emotion. Then he whispered in a hoarse voice, "You did it, kid."

"*We* did it, Henry."

"I guess we did, Bryan, and this is only the beginning for you, believe me." The old man smiled feebly, joking, "I'm sure Ted Grover will be pleased to hear the good news, we should send him an e-mail or something!"

"Ted *who*?" I deadpanned. Henry laughed softly.

We chatted for a few minutes about my schedule for the rest of the summer, but Henry's eyes kept closing. He was exhausted. Finally he sighed, "Bryan, I want to talk to you but I'm just too tired right now." Henry was a stubborn old man who never admitted stuff like that. So when he told me he was too tired to talk I got pretty nervous.

I called up Mike Scully when I left the hospital. I needed to get back onto the tennis court and try to put Henry's condition out of my mind. Mike met me at The Courts an hour later, where I delivered the news about the nationals to him. He couldn't have been more excited. He said it was like reliving his dreams all over again. I was happy and grateful that Mike was now a part of my team. We ended up playing three grueling sets that afternoon, and I actually managed to take the second set from him. When we were finished playing, I went back to the hospital to visit Henry.

CHAPTER THIRTEEN

FROM COURAGE TO KALAMAZOO

Henry had barely touched his dinner when I walked in. Elizabeth was concerned; he was supposed to be taking it as easy as possible because his condition was so frail. Henry seemed to read her mind as he said, "Liz, I need to talk to Bryan. It's important."

She looked at him and smiled, "Fine, but not too long, all right, guys?" She stood up and patted me on the head, taking the dinner tray with her as she left. Henry clicked the remote to shut off the TV as I took a seat in the chair by the bed. Before he spoke to me, he coughed and struggled for breath. There was a solemn tone to his voice as he said, "Bryan, we have a lot to be proud of. Your tennis has come such a long way."

"Yeah, Henry, because you showed me how this game

is supposed to be played."

"Well, maybe, but you have something extra that can't be taught. Johnny had it too. Part of it is simply a pure love of the game. Whether it was a practice match at a park, or the finals of the Southern California Sectionals, all of it was special to Johnny."

"That's kinda how I feel."

"I know it, you're very similar to him in that regard. That's why I want you to remember to embrace every single moment, even if it's while shaking hands after losing a match. Because you know what?" Henry took another breath before finishing his thought, "There will always be another day, another chance to reach for your dreams. Johnny didn't get the chance, but you will." Henry shook his head and smiled. "You've worked hard for this, Bryan. Remember what I once told you? It's a long way from Courage to Kalamazoo. Well, you've earned your ticket."

"I'm scared, Henry. It's a whole new ball game now."

"You wouldn't be human if you weren't scared." The old man spoke slowly and deliberately, "You'll be playing some unbelievable guys out there. But you are every bit as good as they are, you just have to believe it." He looked deep into my eyes and told me, "There's going to be a period of adjustment that might shake your confidence. But keep your head up, because you do belong with them."

"Okay, Henry, I hear you."

"Good, kid, because I can't predict how long it will take you to get up to their level. It might take all of one match, or maybe the whole summer. But I can assure you that there's going to be a time, a moment, when it all comes together for you. And when it happens, don't analyze or question it. It's like a wave, and I want you to ride it as long and as far as you can."

The door opened and Elizabeth walked in, "Henry, it's time for you to rest."

"Soon, Liz. I need a few more minutes."

Elizabeth sighed, and then smiled, "You'll never change, will you, old man?"

"Too late to change now."

She looked at us and said, "Five more minutes." Then she walked out of the room.

"Bryan, pour me a little water, please." Filling a cup from the pitcher by the bed, I put it to Henry's lips and tilted it slightly, then a little more.

"Thanks, kid." He struggled mightily to clear his throat enough to speak. "Listen, no matter what happens, hang in there and keep your head up. Don't be intimidated by a reputation, or by how many titles a guy has. You don't go to a national tournament to make a respectable appearance, you go to lay it all on the line." Henry paused, clearing his throat again. I could see that speaking was very difficult for him. I started to suggest that we call it a night, but he waved me off, "I'm fine. Now, in August, when you get to Kalamazoo, I want you to introduce yourself to one of my oldest friends, a fellow by the name of Charley Morrison. He's there every year and you'll have no trouble finding him. Give him my regards, will you please?"

"Sure, Henry." My eyes started to get watery. "Any-

117

way, you'll be there with me by then, you can say hello to him yourself."

Henry smiled, "I don't think so, kid." Tears welled up in my eyes as I felt Henry's hand squeezing mine. He coughed and I squeezed his hand a little tighter. "Bryan, come closer to me, this is important." I moved my head very close to his. "Remember when you asked me about your dad but I wanted to stay out of it?" After Dad showed up for my tennis match I had asked Henry for advice, because I still wasn't convinced about trusting my father.

"Sure I remember," I replied.

"Well, what I wanted to tell you is that life is just like a tennis match. Your dad's first serve was a fault, he messed up. But you've got to let him have a second crack at it. Remember, Bryan," Henry joked weakly, "you're only as good as your second serve." Henry smiled again, "Look at my life, Bryan. Coaching you, well it was my second serve, my second chance." The old man looked directly into my eyes and said, "Everything makes perfect sense to me now."

A few tears rolled down my cheeks and I knew exactly what I had to do with my father.

"I'll give him another chance, Henry, I promise. And I'll make sure to say hello to your friend at Kalamazoo." I was getting very emotional now.

"All right, Bryan, you should be getting on home before Elizabeth gets mad at both of us."

"Okay, Henry. I'll be back tomorrow, though." As I turned and walked toward the door, I was suddenly transfixed, overcome with emotion. Somehow, I knew at that precise moment that I would never see Henry again. My eyes were full of tears, and as my hand touched the doorknob, I turned around to look at him one last time. The old man was staring right at me with a gentle, tranquil expression. Then he slowly held out his hand. I rushed over to the bed and hugged my teacher. I was crying openly now.

"Don't be sad, kid. Everything's going to work out for you, you'll see."

"Henry, I want to tell you th…that—" I was fumbling for the right words.

"It's all right, Bryan, I know what you want to say. You remind me so much of Johnny. I never got over the hurt of losing him until you came along. For fifty years I've regretted that I never had a chance to tell him just one thing. I don't want to miss this chance with you, too." Henry paused. "I love you, Bryan."

The funeral was a week later. It was a small affair, but it was very tasteful. I cried, as did Elizabeth, but it was comforting to have the closure of celebrating Henry's life with family and a few close friends. I considered shelving my plans for the summer, but my mom encouraged me to go forward. She explained that losing Henry was something I would never fully recover from, but I would have to move on with my life. She said Henry would want it that way.

Henry's words about an adjustment period had been prophetic. My first two national tournaments ended quickly, with convincing dismissals handed down by far more experienced players. Finally, in my third tournament, I won a match, beating a kid from South Carolina 6-3 in the third set. It was satisfying to notch my first victory in national competition, although I quickly fell in the second round, 6-2, 6-3. But I was starting to find my groove, winning two matches in the consolation before being eliminated.

Things went ahead as scheduled, and at the end of July our airplane roared its way toward the Kalamazoo/Battle Creek International Airport in Michigan. Kalamazoo was my fourth national tournament, and the site of the oldest and most revered junior tournament in America, the USTA Super National Hard Court Championships.

After the plane landed, Mom, Brandon, and I made our way through the terminal to a courtesy bus that would take us to our hotel. As we walked, I looked at the numerous signs and posters that were hanging from the walls. One said, "Welcome to Kalamazoo, host of the Super National Championships for over fifty years." I felt a shiver run down my spine as Henry's words entered my mind: *"It's a long way from Courage to Kalamazoo."*

Two days later, I was so nervous I thought I was going to be sick. Just one short year ago I had been playing small state events in Kansas. Now I was on a tennis court playing my first match ever at the Super National Hard Court Championships! Right after my first serve of the day, my nerves quickly subsided, replaced by a pleasing sense of calm. Now I just wanted to play.

Joe Drucker, my opponent, was very tough, a lefty with an excellent serve and volley. This kid from Berkeley, California, was posing a tremendous challenge, but something strange happened early in the match that changed everything. We were deadlocked at 3-all in the first set, but I had earned my first break point as a result of an errant forehand by Drucker. It was 30-40, and the wiry lefty rushed to the net behind a wide serve that pulled me off the court. I hit a backhand return that stayed up just a little too long, and Drucker expertly hit a crosscourt volley that seemed to be out of my reach. At that instant I had an extraordinary experience. I wondered if my imagination was playing tricks on me, but for a moment it felt like I was back home in Courage, playing a practice match, with Henry perched at his customary spot in the window upstairs. *If I don't chase that ball down, Henry's gonna give me an earful!*

Without hesitation I gave an all-out sprint for a ball that was heading for a comfortable landing near the far side-line. Seeing that I couldn't quite get there in time, I lunged at the ball the way a third baseman dives to stop a rocket down the line. In mid-air, I swung as hard as I could—and to my surprise I nailed a topspin forehand right up the line, just out of reach of a startled Drucker! It was the greatest shot that had ever exploded off my racket.

Once that happened, a change took place, like when I'd realized that I could compete with the best players from my own section. I knew that I belonged here. My tennis game was solid, there were no holes to fill, no gaps to bridge. Henry had often talked about a moment, a single point, a shot, something that would indicate that I had arrived. I was sure that I had just played out that point, and hit the shot of my life. Suddenly, I understood that the old man had instilled something in my psyche that gave me the audacity to continually reach for higher levels without fear of failure. My new frame of mind carried me straight through to a decisive 6-4, 6-3 victory over a tough opponent. That win broke the ice for me, which was important because I had previously felt quite intimidated just being at Kalamazoo.

Unlike me, there were some players in this tournament whose reputations had truly preceded them. Although the top seed, Danny Gold, was in a class of his own, there were no weak links among the top four or five guys. They were simply the elite sixteen-year-olds in America. But perhaps I was just too awestruck to realize that I was hitting the ball as well as anyone there, and that nobody had a stronger will to win. With three national tournaments already under my belt, I had quickly gained a world of experience, which was teaching me how to win at this level. Maybe I was an anonymous kid from a weak section, but I was peaking at exactly the right time.

CHAPTER FOURTEEN

THE LEGACY OF KALAMAZOO

The next day I dismissed Michael Anderson of Los Angeles, California, 6-2 in the third. Although the conditions were hot and humid, both of us were extremely fit and up to the challenge. Anderson, who stood only five-feet-eight, was a pesky baseliner who hit with two hands off both sides. His serve wasn't much, but his highly effective game revolved around steadiness and control. He possessed the stamina and mental toughness to stay out on the court for a week, if that's what it took to win a match.

But after the first two sets were decided by tiebreakers, I was able to break the affair wide open with a torrential on-slaught of pressure. I simply overpowered Anderson, imposing my will on a very capable opponent who, physically, was not my equal.

That evening I was on the phone with Mike Scully, telling him all about the match with Anderson. I also had some significant news to report. "Mike, remember I told you last night that the winner of my match gets Bobby Jackson?"

"Sure."

"Well, Jackson was upset today."

"Wow, the third seed out in the second round! Who'd he lose to?"

"Some guy from Chicago named Eddie Binder. I've never even heard of him."

"Well, Bryan, nobody's heard of you either, but you've already made it to the round of thirty-two. So don't get complacent. This guy Binder just beat the third seed, which means he's gonna have some serious momentum."

"You're right, Mike." I smiled, knowing that I had lucked out by having Mike as my new coach. Henry cared so much about me that he made sure a successor was in place to help me carry on! "Oh hey, Mike, guess what? I saw a photo of you on the Wall of Champions, you're a Kalamazoo legend!"

Mike chuckled, "Let's not go overboard. I did win the sixteens there one year, but I never quite got over the top in the eighteens. But I'm happy to hear that I'm still remembered there."

"For sure, but dude, what was up with your hair back then?" I kidded.

"Please, don't remind me," Mike laughed. "And speaking of bad hair, I have a message for you. I was at The Courts today and I saw your good buddy, that clown Jimmy Ellis. He wished you luck—and he said that even if you end up being ranked number one in the nation, he'll *still* tax your butt on the tennis court!"

I laughed, "Good ol' Jimmy. He'll never change."

The next day, I faced unseeded Eddie Binder, a scrappy competitor who had a knack for frustrating adversaries with his completely unorthodox game. He didn't hit the ball very solidly; he hit a lot of junk. Warming up, I thought, *This guy is not that good.* But he had obviously been good enough to send the third seed reeling.

It seemed like Binder hadn't hit one clean shot, but just like that, he was up a set and a break. I had tried to counter the junk by pounding every ball, but that strategy was playing right into the hands of my resourceful opponent.

Henry had always advocated the concept of changing a game plan if it wasn't working. So, out of desperation, I started easing up on my groundstrokes and going to heavy topspin instead. This subtle change had a real effect on Binder. No longer able to rely on my pace, he was forced to create his own. That wasn't nearly as desirable for him, leading to a shift in momentum as the match slowly began to turn. By the time it was 3-all in the third, the contest had become a test of courage as well as skill. Both of us were worn out, our gas tanks depleted by two hours of unflinching combat. I felt like I was ready to collapse.

But this situation wasn't much different from those countless sessions when Henry simply wouldn't let me quit. I pictured the old man yelling at me, reciting a familiar anecdote about how hard players used to work in the old days. The memory brought a smile to my face—and it also gave me the extra boost I direly needed.

Shrugging off my fatigue, I stepped up to meet the challenge. Knowing I would have to outlast my opponent, I became determined to stay out there as long as necessary. Binder continued to fight; but finally, twenty-five agonizing minutes later, he succumbed, 7-5 in the third.

That night, I was exhausted, but I felt a rush of exhilaration. I was still in! I had the next day off, and then I would play my round of sixteen match on Wednesday against the number thirteen seed, Jason Turner, of Copper Mountain, Colorado.

I tried to keep my mind off that match and appreciate what I had already accomplished. I told myself that no matter what happened next, nothing could change the fact that I had reached the round of sixteen of the Super National Championships. Many great players and future champions had stamped their imprint on this legendary tournament. Now I, too, had become a small part of the legacy of Kalamazoo.

After breakfast the next morning I took the hotel shuttle over to Kalamazoo College, the site of the tournament. My mom wanted to take Brandon to get a haircut and then do a little sightseeing, so we made plans to meet up again around noon. I had made arrangements to hit later that afternoon, but first there was some business I wanted to attend to. In the excitement of the tournament, I had forgotten to look up Henry's old friend, Charley Morrison.

As Henry had predicted, it wasn't very hard to locate Morrison, a popular sportswriter who had covered the Super Nationals for more than forty years. He was retired, but he still came out every year to enjoy the tennis. I found him relaxing at an outdoor table, sipping iced tea as he leisurely read the newspaper.

"Excuse me, Mr. Morrison?"

"Yes?" The old sportswriter put down the paper and looked up.

"My name is Bryan Berry, and an old friend of yours, Henry Johnson, asked me to look you up when I got to Kalamazoo. He wanted me to give you his regards."

Morrison's face lit up like a bright light bulb, "Henry Johnson! I haven't spoken to him in years. Sit down, son, please!"

"Thanks," I said, putting my tennis bag on the ground and sitting down across from Morrison.

"Now, how do you know Henry?"

"He was my coach for the last couple of years. He just passed away about two months ago." It was still an incredibly painful thing to say.

"Oh my, I'm so sorry to hear that. They never made them any finer than Henry, that's for sure. Our friendship dates back to California, when he was one of the best-known teaching pros on the West Coast. But he stopped coaching years and years ago. Did you say he was *your* coach?"

"Yes, sir, he sure was. He hadn't done it in a long time, but all I know is that he made me into a tennis player. I wouldn't be sitting here right now if it weren't for him."

"That sounds like the Henry I knew. Understood the game better than anyone I've ever seen, and I've seen 'em all. Nobody could get more out of a player than he could." Morrison smiled, "Back in our day, Henry was in such demand that parents of potential tennis stars would offer him money and all kinds of things just to take a look at their kid. A Hollywood producer even offered to put Henry in the movies!"

I tried to envision it. I joked, "Henry could have been a movie star!"

"Henry could have been anything, but he gave it all up." Morrison shrugged his shoulders. "It's a real shame, too. If certain things had gone differently for him, I believe that he would have achieved legendary stature as a coach." Morrison's face was stoic, but his voice was colored with emotion.

"You mean…if Johnny hadn't died?"

Morrison looked at me for a long moment. "Yes, that changed everything for Henry. Did he tell you a lot about him?" I nodded. "Johnny Matthews had the prettiest game I ever saw in my life. There's no doubt in my mind that he was destined for stardom. What a tragedy." Morrison shuddered. "And what a blow to Henry," he added.

"They were real close, huh?"

"Yes," Morrison said. "I'm sure you gathered that by the way Henry talked about him, right?"

"Yeah, it was like he was talking about his own kid."

Morrison took a long sip of his iced tea and changed the subject. "Now, son, tell me about yourself. Any protégé of Henry's must be good. He always knew talent when he saw it."

So I proceeded to tell the whole story, beginning with the first Courage Open, when Henry approached me after the loss to Grover. Morrison listened with rapt attention as I related all of the subsequent events in rich detail. Discussing my relationship with Henry was quite therapeutic and Morrison seemed to understand. For him, hearing this elaborate story about Henry Johnson was like being reunited with a long-lost friend. He laughed uproariously at some of the episodes I recounted, and he jumped in with several anecdotes of his own. When I got to the part about Henry getting sick and then suffering the heart attack, Morrison's eyes were moist. But he seemed enthralled by my account of Henry's confinement to a sick bed while I battled my way through the Missouri Valley Supers Circuit.

"Son, I'm so happy he lived long enough to hear that you were going to the nationals. I *know* how much that meant to him. You gave him a wonderful gift."

I was speechless for a moment, awestruck at the notion that I might have given Henry so much. All I knew for certain was that he had given me everything. "I sure appreciate hearing you say that, Mr. Morrison, because I always figured that nothing could ever make up for Johnny never getting to the nationals."

"Bryan, based on what you've told me, there's no doubt in my mind that you were as dear to Henry as Johnny was. And that puts you in very good company."

"Thank you, sir."

Both of us stood up, and Morrison looked at me thoughtfully as we shook hands. "You're a Henry Johnson disciple, there's no question about it. I'm gonna watch your match tomorrow. Win or lose, wherever he is right now, I bet Henry is real proud of you."

CHAPTER FIFTEEN

THE KID FROM COURAGE

If someone had asked me to explain what was happening, I probably would have been at a loss for words. It was like a dream. Henry spoke about a moment when everything would come together, likening it to the momentum of a wave. This was more like a tidal wave, growing with dramatic speed.

After I won two more matches, I had become the talk of the Super National Championships. Local newspaper articles captured the unfolding story with headlines like "From 'The Courts' to the 'Zoo—Unknown Takes Nationals by Storm" and "The Kid from Courage Wins Again." There were interviews, even an appearance on a local television news show. Things were getting out of hand.

In the round of sixteen, I had eliminated Jason Turner, a left-handed player with amazing talent but very little mental toughness. He reminded me of Jimmy Ellis in some ways. Although Turner hit some of the greatest shots that I had ever seen, he also missed a lot of routine ones. I had established my game plan quickly: hang around, keep the ball in the court, and fight for every point. The contrast of styles made for some very entertaining tennis. I was a smart, aggressive baseliner who came in on every good opportunity, while Turner was a flamboyant, erratic player who was extremely capable of hitting a spectacular shot at any moment. But he didn't hit nearly enough of them as I outsteadied him 6-4, 7-5.

That win thrust me into the quarters, where I beat the number six seed, Seth Green, 6-3 in the third. A rock-solid serve-and-volleyer, Green found himself matched up against an opponent who was returning as well as anyone he'd faced all year. As a result, he started going for too much on his serve, which caused him to start missing. The sixteen-year-old from Arizona fought valiantly, but he simply couldn't find his way, finally succumbing to my pressure. The points were fierce and competitive, but the truth was that I was playing unconscious tennis.

It was now Friday, a day off for me. The semis were the next day, so my plans were to relax, and then hit lightly in the afternoon. I definitely needed some rest because my body was starting to feel a little weary from all the tennis I had played over the last few months. Brandon and I hung out for a couple of hours at Kalamazoo College, where I had become something of a local celebrity. People were actually coming up to talk to me or wish me luck, and a few even asked for autographs. It was quite an experience for two small-town kids who were not used to this kind of attention. Both of us had a blast. But the bigger surprise was waiting when we got back to the hotel. We walked in the lobby and standing there, with a wide grin on his face, was our dad! Brandon ran over and jumped on him, talking excitedly in between hugs.

Dad stared across at me. Looking into his eyes, all I could think about was Henry and what he'd said to me before he passed. I knew it was time to give Dad a chance to crack a winning second serve. I ran over to him and hugged him tightly. I didn't want to let go. "I'm not angry about anything anymore," I told him. "Let's just start over right now." When I spoke those words it was like a giant weight had been lifted from my back.

Dad was a little choked up. "Thank you, Bryan. I won't let you down this time."

This time, I believed him.

The next day I was on the stadium court facing the number two seed, Shawn Robertson, a sixteen-year-old from Atlanta. Robertson was an explosive baseliner who hit the ball with fierce topspin off both sides. He was a superlative athlete who was very sound mentally—all the trademarks of a prime-time tennis player.

Curiously, I wasn't especially nervous as the match began. Obviously I realized that I was appearing in front of the largest crowd of my life, but I was surprisingly serene. I told myself that even a love and love thrashing wouldn't detract from my notable accomplishments. I was in the semis of Kalamazoo, having beaten two seeds along the way.

Ironically, it was Robertson who was nervous. Currently

the number two player in the nation, he had enjoyed an out-standing year with one national title already under his belt. But in addition to a tender left ankle, which he had injured earlier in the week, he was aware that he was facing an opponent who had utterly nothing to lose. Robertson also knew that the crowd would throw all of its high-spirited support in my direction because I was the underdog.

Although he was playing at less than one hundred percent due to his injury, Robertson was still a talented and dangerous tennis player. We were thrilling the crowd with artistic rallies, punctuated by sensational winners. As the first set went into a tiebreaker, the match was completely up for grabs.

As Robertson had correctly anticipated, the crowd was vocal in its support for me. But as a very experienced tournament player, he wasn't bothered by it at all. He was having enough trouble on the court without worrying about anything else. He tried to forget about his ankle, which was hurting, and go for it in the tiebreaker.

But I was psyched and ready. Before I served the first point of the breaker, Henry's familiar words entered my mind: *The game that gets you there won't win it for you.* The tiebreaker turned out to be one of the highlights of the entire tournament. Both of us raised our games to produce some magnificent tennis. With Henry's words dancing in my head, I was hitting the ball as hard as I could. As for Robertson, he had decided that his ankle wouldn't be able to withstand too much more of this furious pace. He had to win this set.

By the time it was 11-all in this dramatic tiebreaker, both of us had saved three set points. After Robertson drew a short return from me with a blazing first serve, he charged the net behind a big topspin forehand. The ball landed in the corner but stayed up just a little too long. I got there and completely fooled him with a looping crosscourt backhand. To the delight of the crowd, I now had a set point on my own serve.

I had been hitting my first serve with tremendous pace for the entire match. This time, however, I spun it high to Robertson's backhand and rushed in behind it. Robertson, who was standing behind the baseline, didn't have time to catch the ball on the rise. Instead, he was forced to let it come up to him. The result was a chipped return that floated lazily through the air. I pounced on it and easily put the volley away.

Robertson was disheartened, to say the least. Had he pulled out the first set, his experience might have helped him squeak out a victory. But now, with a bum ankle, he was down a set to a guy who was obviously willing to stay out there all day if necessary.

Shawn Robertson fought bravely for a little while longer, but he was eventually subdued, 7-6, 6-3. The Kid from Courage was in the finals of the Super National Championships!

From the moment I walked off the court, it seemed like everyone in the world wanted a piece of me. They wanted interviews, pictures, and appearances. Some college coaches handed me their business cards, as did representatives from various clothing and shoe companies. But I was grateful that my family was with me. They swept me out of there as quickly as possible, and we sequestered ourselves at the hotel for the rest of the day. Mom intercepted the numerous phone calls that were coming in, while I tried to relax and keep my mind off the finals. I made only two telephone calls, one to Mike Scully and the other to Charley Morrison.

The next day I tried to appear composed and relaxed as I loosened up. But it was overwhelming to hear the chair umpire's voice reverberate throughout Stowe Stadium's venerable center court, "And to my right, a player who has left an indelible mark on these championships. He has beaten three seeds to become only the fourth unseeded player in the history of Kalamazoo to reach the finals. From Courage, Kansas: Bryan Berry!" The crowd spontaneously responded with a thunderous standing ovation, which sent chills up and down my spine. I felt a surge of nervous energy as I took a quick look around the huge stadium. What an awesome sight! Thousands of tennis fans had gathered here on this beautiful summer afternoon to see if my Cinderella story had enough magic left in it to pull off one of the greatest upsets in the history of junior tennis.

My opponent today was none other than Danny Gold, undeniably the best sixteen-year-old in the United States. Watching him warm up, it wasn't hard to understand why *Tennis Monthly* had dubbed him the "Golden Child" of American junior tennis. Gold was an imposing figure, a wondrously skilled player who seemed to have every shot in the book. There was an aura of invincibility about him that was downright intimidating.

"Ladies and gentlemen, this match will be two out of three sets. Mr. Gold has won the toss and he has elected to serve first. Players ready?" The umpire looked around for a second. "Play!"

The first point of the match showcased some very impressive tennis. Both of us were punishing the ball during a long, hard-fought baseline rally. Finally, a short ball gave me the opening I was looking for. I moved forward, pounding my approach shot crosscourt as I charged to the net. Gold raced to the corner, and on the dead run he passed me with a screaming forehand up the line. The crowd burst into applause as I glanced at my opponent for an instant. *Oh, man, you really are as good as everybody says!*

Gold easily held serve and we switched sides. I was determined to establish myself with an aggressive service game, eager to show Gold that this match would be vigorously contested. I opened up by cranking my heavy first serve, a bullet that found the line. Fifteen-love. I went for it again, but Gold was ready this time. Catching the ball early, he pressed forward behind a scorching return that forced me out of position. He completed the point by punching a shoulder high volley into the open court.

Three points later Gold had the first break chance of the match. After my first serve caught the tape and fell back, Gold crept inside the baseline, looking to hit and come in. His chipped approach shot stayed low and I tried to counter with a topspin lob, but it wasn't nearly deep enough. Gold effortlessly put it away, and—just like that—it was 2-love.

After Gold held again, I started to feel a little bit discouraged. It was still early, but this was the exact beginning I had feared. Under normal circumstances I wouldn't be too concerned about finding myself down a quick break. But there was nothing normal about this match, not with the brilliant

Danny Gold on the other side of the net. I ordered myself to stay mentally tough and battle for every point.

Although the tennis continued to be highly entertaining, there was no mystery surrounding the outcome of the first set. With an eloquent display of raw power and skill, Danny Gold prevailed easily, 6-2. The top seed was clearly in the driver's seat, and it didn't seem as though he had any intention of letting up.

Like me, Gold was a kid from a small town, a disciplined tennis player who was known as a no-nonsense hard worker on the court. He was a gifted athlete who had also won at Kalamazoo the previous year, a remarkable feat at the age of fifteen. Now he was on course for back-to-back crowns, and he seemed determined that nothing would stand in his way.

The second set began with solid tennis as we stayed on serve through the first three games. But Gold suddenly started returning more aggressively, taking some calculated chances that paid off in a big way. I tried to fend him off, but finally, on his third break point, he hit a beautiful drop volley to seize the game. After holding serve, he was in control with a commanding 4-1 lead.

I tried to gather my thoughts as I sat down and took a long swig of water. There was no getting around the fact that the match was slipping away from me. It certainly wasn't a disgrace to lose to the best player in the nation, especially considering how heavily he had been favored. But I was not interested in simply making a respectable showing. I had come here today with a purpose, but a quick glance up at the huge scoreboard told the story loud and clear:

	1	2	3
D. Gold	6	4	
B. Berry	2	1	

I considered changing tactics. But to what? *If I hit and come in, I get passed. It's impossible to outsteady this guy, and I sure don't want to give him a chance to attack the net.* What would Henry advise at a time like this? My mind wandered back to those marathon practice sessions, where Henry's strong will was the driving force behind our improbable quest. The old man had taught me to believe in myself and to believe that no obstacle was too great to overcome.

I also thought about Johnny—a kid whose outlook on life was so positive that it inspired everyone around him. I recalled Henry's words about how Johnny appreciated everything about tennis, from the practice matches to the important tournaments. I knew that Johnny would have been thrilled to be here right now, even down a set and 4-1. Win or lose, he would have treasured the moment and welcomed the challenge.

After defiantly taking one more look at the scoreboard, I blocked everything else out of my mind and began to fight—harder than I had ever fought before. Summoning my entire reserve of strength and resolve, I played each point as though the championship hinged upon it. Slowly, I started traveling the long road back. I got the break back, and then used every last ounce of energy in my body to get the second set into a tiebreaker, which I miraculously pulled out, 8-6.

The crowd had embraced me as their very own. A kid

from the heartland of America, who hadn't even played sectionals the year before, had captivated the people. Everyone seemed to have something to say about me.

Even Charley Morrison had gotten into the act. He had come out of retirement to write a story for the *Kalamazoo Gazette* entitled "From Courage to Kalamazoo." Morrison had plucked the title from conversations between Henry and me, as related by me. In the article, Morrison chronicled my rise from an ordinary player to a force at the most prestigious USTA junior tournament in America. He did so by interweaving my life with Johnny's, portraying two kids, more than fifty years apart, who were linked together by one thing—the presence of a cherished mentor who guided them with strength and wisdom, helping them to accomplish things that exceeded their wildest dreams. Not only did the town eat it up, but papers in Los Angeles, Chicago, New York, and, of course, Kansas, also picked up the story.

The enthusiasm of the crowd was helping me generate the little energy I had remaining. This was my seventh match in nine days, and by the time it was 1-all in the third, I was completely spent. After being shocked by my second set heroics, Gold willed himself to regain the momentum. He broke and then held for a 3-1 lead.

As the match started to draw to a conclusion, the crowd didn't decrease its support for me. Instead, the fans got even louder. With defeat almost a certainty, I was still trying as hard as my body would possibly let me. I had cramped up, left to rely upon sheer will to run around the court. With Gold serving at 5-2, I refused to die, sending the game to seven thrilling deuces. I saved five championship points along the way.

When Gold finally put the championship away with a booming overhead, the crowd stood up in unison and cheered with admiration. I was so drained that I could barely stand up, but I forced myself to make my way forward with my hand extended. But Gold didn't shake it. He jumped over the net, and without saying one word he put his arm around my shoulder. The roar of the crowd reached a crescendo as we walked over to the sidelines together and took a bow.

Everyone in the stadium felt as though they had witnessed something incredible. Ten days earlier, I had been a complete unknown, an anonymous face in an illustrious field. Now, as the tournament was coming to an end, and Danny Gold was fulfilling his expectations, everyone knew the name Bryan Berry. I had given Danny Gold a rousing challenge and I was sure we would face off again in the future.

As they were setting up the trophy presentation, I was sitting in my chair at courtside, exhausted, my face buried in a towel. The flock of photographers who had gathered around me captured the scene with a hail of clicks from their cameras. I was crying tears that were a mixture of happiness and sadness. There was the realization that my game had unlimited potential, pointing to a future full of promise. But all I could think about was my friend and coach, Henry. *Look what we did together, you and me. We went the distance and we're still standing. Oh, man, Henry, I'd give anything to have you here right now to hear this applause.*

I looked up from the towel and gazed straight up to the sky, where the sun was majestically starting a slow descent. I stared at the beautiful sight for a few moments, and then I looked into the stands, to the section where my family was sitting. My mom was juggling a camcorder in one hand and a disposable camera in another, while wiping away tears at the same time. I waved to her. Brandon was jumping up and down and giving me the thumbs-up sign, and apparently letting everyone seated around him know that *he* was Bryan Berry's brother. And Dad was standing tall and straight with a proud look on his face as he stared directly at me. I looked at him and smiled, thumping my chest and pointing at him. He did the same and it made me feel like I was the one who had just won Kalamazoo. Just one more victory that Henry had helped me notch.

I missed my coach dearly, and I knew that nothing would ever be the same without him. But I also knew that the spirit of our friendship was like an unbreakable bond that would always remain a part of me. I was now carrying the torch—forever—for myself, for Johnny, and most of all, for Henry.

I wondered what inimitable "Henryism" would be delivered if the old man were standing there with me at that moment. I smiled, and then laughed out loud. Probably something like, "Okay, kid, lose the tears and pull yourself together. Let's get done with this ceremony and get back home. We've got a lot of work to do."

TEST YOURSELF...ARE YOU A PROFESSIONAL READER?

Chapter 1: The King of Courage High

Why is Bryan tempted to accept Jimmy's invitation to go to the football game? What is his reason for declining?

Why did Bryan move to Courage? How did he become interested in tennis?

Who is Henry Johnson? Recount two of his colorful tennis stories.

ESSAY

Nothing in the world is more important to Bryan than his tennis. Detail a sport or any other activity (music, writing, science, etc.) that you are passionate about. Explain how you grew interested in this sport/activity and why it is important to you.

Chapter 2: The Courage Open

After Bryan's first-round match, he talks to his mom and reminisces about a match from the previous year. What happened and why does Bryan suddenly turn quiet?

Who is Mike Scully? List some of his accomplishments.

What stroke of luck enables Bryan to squeak out a victory in his second-round match against Randy Kaplan?

ESSAY

As he studies the draw to assess the match-ups, Jimmy Ellis self-assuredly projects that he will easily reach the quarterfinals of the tournament. Do you consider yourself to be a confident person? When you are faced with a difficult situation like an important test or an athletic contest, do you look forward to the challenge or do you dread the very thought of it? Explain your answer.

Chapter 3: Afraid to Lose

Ted Grover lives up to his infamous reputation by pulling his usual antics at the end of the second set against Bryan. Detail Grover's actions and how they alter the outcome of the match.

What happens when Bryan is dejectedly sitting by himself after his gut-wrenching defeat to Ted Grover?

According to Mr. Johnson, Bryan needs to start from scratch with some of his strokes, even if he loses some matches in the process. Why does the Old Man Johnson think it's a mistake for juniors to be focused solely upon winning?

ESSAY

Bryan is amazed that Henry Johnson, an old man who is supposedly "out of touch," has so much apparent wisdom and understanding. Who is the person of a distant generation in your life (grandparent, teacher, or family friend) that you can relate to despite the age difference? Describe your relationship with this person.

Chapter 4: Coach

In his response to Mr. Johnson's question, what does Bryan reveal about his goals in tennis?

After Bryan loses his practice match to Jimmy, Bryan tells him that he has been working on his tennis with Mr. Johnson. What is Jimmy's reaction? Why does Jimmy warn Bryan to be careful about learning the game from Mr. Johnson?

Bryan impulsively asks Mr. Johnson to become his coach, even though he knows people will question his decision. Why is having Mr. Johnson as a coach such a huge gamble?

ESSAY

As Bryan begins to train with Mr. Johnson, his match and tournament results do nothing to validate his association with the old man. Detail a time in your life when you were confronted with a situation where you did something that everybody disagreed with. How did you deal with the criticism? Would you have made the same decision a second time?

Chapter 5: Dad's Back

When Bryan comes home from school and sees his dad's car parked on his driveway, he isn't shocked. Why not? What had he confided to his mom about these unexpected visits?

What big announcement does Bryan's dad make in this chapter? What hopes of Bryan's are dashed as a result?

While his mom is in court, what does Bryan daydream about in class? Why does the prospect of living with his dad scare him?

ESSAY

Are your parents divorced, or are the parents of any of your friends divorced? If so, how does this situation make you feel and what kind of adjustments do you (or your friends) have to make? What advice would you give to other kids who are faced with a similar situation?

Chapter 6: Johnny Matthews

In response to Bryan's question, what does Mr. Johnson say about how he became acquainted with Johnny Matthews? What does Mr. Johnson tell Bryan about Johnny's father?

Detail the incident that caused the untimely death of Johnny Matthews.

According to Mr. Johnson, what similarities exist between Bryan and Johnny?

ESSAY

Bryan is awestruck when he sees all the trophies at Mr. Johnson's house. Have you ever won a trophy, an award, or earned a flawless report card? How did this honor make you feel? Detail the character traits that you displayed to earn this distinction.

Chapter 7: A Loony Old Quack

Although Bryan's dad seems sincere in expressing a desire to reconnect with his children, explain why Bryan is skeptical. What does his mom encourage him to do in response to this situation?

Why do the obnoxious club members give Bryan a hard time, and how does Bryan deal with them?

What causes Bryan to miss the Missouri Valley Supers Circuit tournament, and how does Henry respond to the situation?

ESSAY

A difficult day is made even worse for Bryan when the club members ridicule him. Describe a time when a bunch of kids ganged up on you or someone you know and called you (or your friends) names? Describe what happened and how you/ others dealt with the situation.

Chapter 8: Summer Vacation

Describe the professional sporting event that Bryan character- izes as one of the highlights of his summer.

On the first day of school, Bryan reflects on his trip to Los Angeles. What did he and his dad do together? What did the two of them talk about?

What story does Henry tell Bryan concerning Sam "Grand Slam" Diamond?

ESSAY

Bryan's exciting summer is capped off by a great trip to Los Angeles. Describe the best trip that you have ever taken in your life. Where did you go? Who were you with? What did you do? What was the highlight of the trip?

Chapter 9: The Party

What does Bryan suspect about the punch at the party and how does this revelation lead to a strong dose of peer pressure?

What dramatic event occurs when Bryan bumps into Adam

Parker at the party?

What are the ramifications of Jimmy's actions at the party?

ESSAY

Bryan behaves uncharacteristically at the party because of the pressure he feels to fit in, even though most of the people there— other than Jimmy— aren't even his friends. Detail a situation in which you were dared to do something that you really didn't want to do. In retrospect, was your decision the right one? Would you do the same again or would you have the courage and resolve to stand up for your principles?

Chapter 10: The Return of the Courage Open

As he warms up with his nemesis, Ted Grover, Bryan realizes that there are many differences between this year's and last year's match. What are they?

After defeating Ted Grover, Bryan gives a very personal and heartfelt gift to Henry. What is the gift? What is the significance of giving this present to Henry on this particular day?

What note does Bryan read during his match with Mike Scully? What change takes place as a result?

ESSAY

For the first time in his life, Bryan is able to turn in a sparkling performance at the Courage Open in front of his family, coach, and many other people. Have you ever had the chance to do something special in front of everybody (act in a play, give a speech, compete in an athletic event, etc.)? How did this situation make you feel? Did people give you compliments on your accomplishment? And if you haven't yet experienced such, is this something that you are willing to work hard for, even if it will require your maximum efforts? Explain.

Chapter 11: Preparing for Battle

Explain what the Missouri Valley Supers Circuit is, and what reward awaits the top six participants.

What leads to Mike Scully "pinch-hitting" for Henry as Bryan prepares for the Missouri Valley Supers Circuit? Why does Mike embrace the opportunity?

In the match against Craig Schroeder, Bryan faces the most dangerous situation any tennis player can ever face on the tennis court. What is that situation and how does Bryan handle it?

ESSAY

Although his tennis skills have declined, Jimmy Ellis apparently feels happy about his steadily improving grades and the chance to go to a decent college. Describe a difficult period in your life and how you found a way to pull yourself to a more satisfied state. What was causing your unhappiness? What changes did you make to enable yourself to feel better?

Chapter 12: The Final Piece of the Puzzle

Who is sitting in the stands watching Bryan's match with Ricky Segal? Why is the mere sight of this onlooker meaningful to Bryan?

What life-altering event takes place on the very same day that Bryan is scoring his huge win over Segal? What does Bryan do when he receives the news?

List the six players that are endorsed by the selection committee. What is Henry's reaction? What little joke does Henry make about Ted Grover?

ESSAY

Bryan is worried because he knows that Henry is old and obviously very sick. Have you ever visited a member of your family at the hospital and been worried about their well-being? How did this situation make you feel? Explain.

Chapter 13: From Courage to Kalamazoo

What advice does Henry dispense regarding the relationship between Bryan and his dad? How does Henry use the expression "You're only as good as your second serve" to make his point?

What happens when Bryan is getting ready to leave the hospital?

An extraordinary experience occurs during Bryan's match with Joe Drucker. Describe this occurrence and explain what change takes place as a result of such.

ESSAY

Henry reminds Bryan that he had once told him that, "It's a long way from Courage from Kalamazoo." Now that Bryan has accomplished his goal, he and Henry reflect on how far they've come. Detail an obstacle that you've overcome in your life. What did you do and how did this accomplishment make you feel? Explain.

Chapter 14: The Legacy of Kalamazoo

When Bryan finds himself losing to Eddie Binder, what strategy of Henry's does he employ, and what memory brings a smile to his face?

What does Charley Morrison relate to Bryan that detailed how Henry's coaching services were in demand back in the old days? What funny story does Charley tell Bryan about an offer made to Henry by a Hollywood movie producer?

According to Charley Morrison, what gift did Bryan give Henry? How does this awakening make Bryan feel about his friendship with Henry?

ESSAY

At the very brink of exhaustion, Bryan pays tribute to Henry by digging in and going the distance during his match with Eddie Binder. Detail a time in your life when you felt the satisfaction of working above and beyond your means to achieve something (working late at night to finish a school project, winning a game in overtime, etc.). Explain what you did and what gave you the motivation to put forth the extra effort.

Chapter 15: The Kid from Courage

What do Bryan and Brandon do on Bryan's day off before the semifinals, and what surprise awaits them at their hotel?

What had Charley Morrison done to pay tribute to Henry Johnson, which also contributes to the affection the crowd feels toward Bryan?

While waiting for the trophy presentation to begin, what does Bryan see when he looks into the stands, and what happens between him and his dad that makes him think about Henry?

ESSAY

Until Bryan uses the memory of Henry's determination and strong will as a motivating force to mount a comeback, he is clearly in awe of Danny Gold. Detail a situation in which you had to play against an opponent or a team that was much better than you were. Did you lose badly or were you able to mount a fight? Do you remember how this experience felt, and what you learned from your journey? Answer this question by relating your words and experiences to similar examples from Bryan's journey throughout the book.